George Frederic Parsons

Middle ground; Between East and West

A Christmas story

George Frederic Parsons

Middle ground; Between East and West
A Christmas story

ISBN/EAN: 9783743383692

Manufactured in Europe, USA, Canada, Australia, Japa

Cover: Foto ©Andreas Hilbeck / pixelio.de

Manufactured and distributed by brebook publishing software
(www.brebook.com)

George Frederic Parsons

Middle ground; Between East and West

MIDDLE GROUND.

CHAPTER I.

" KILL-ME-QUICK."

On a certain morning, early in the month of May, in a certain year not necessary to specify, the sun, rearing his head above the crests of the Wahsatch Mountains, took a mildly radiant survey of the stretch of hilly country that lay to the westward, and finding nothing very inviting in the barren and lifeless scene, ascended higher, and cast a some-what stronger beam down into a shallow valley, and upon a scattered and confusedly arranged assemblage of tents and rough board shanties.

At that hour, and viewed by that pure, bright, yet soft light, a stranger might have been pardoned for mistaking the innocent-looking place for an encampment of hardy and industrious Mormons, or equally hardy and industrious railroad laborers; for it was situated in the Territory of Utah, and hard by was the yet uncompleted line of the Union Pacific Railroad. But neither the necessities of railroad enterprise, nor the necessities of Brigham Young's followers, accounted for the presence in that sterile valley of those tents and shanties : nor, indeed, is it probable that the stranger, no matter whence he came, would have fallen into either of the mistakes hinted at, had he been aware that the camp was called—Kill-me-Quick.

The day was Sunday, and this fact was indicated at Kill-me-

Quick in a somewhat peculiar manner, viz : by the presence of certain unmistakable evidences that it was the morning after Saturday night. The camp was known far and wide as a particularly lively one—indeed, there were some sanguine spirits who were known to have predicted that if it survived it would shortly rival Cheyenne. On the morning in question its liveliness was of rather a drowsy and befuddled kind, but there were not wanting signs that it had been true to itself, and had fully maintained its character, on the previous evening. From out the entrance of no less than seven tents protruded what looked in the dim light of early morning like black logs, arranged in pairs, but which became revealed, when the sun rose higher, as the pedal extremities of a corresponding number of citizens, whose devotion to the bottle over night had incapacitated them from winning their way further into the interior of their respective domicils.

But the early sun shone on uglier things than the fourteen mud-encrusted boots of the seven oblivious citizens aforementioned. In the center of the little alley, which formed the main and only street, stood a tent erected over and enclosing a rude frame of lumber. It was larger and more ambitious than its fellows, and a canvas sign nailed along its front informed the public that Mr. Richard Bouser was prepared to dispense liquid refreshments of every imaginable description. This place was silent now, and the canvas curtain that served for a door was drawn close. But the thick, pasty mud in front was trampled and stamped as with furiously struggling feet, and within a radius of ten yards lay three citizens who would never again be enrolled among the customers of Mr. Richard Bouser. They all lay with their heads outward, and their feet pointing towards the doorway. They all lay on their backs, their faces white, and set, and rigid, and their eyes glaring unwinkingly at the sun, that stared down in return as though amazed. On their soiled and torn clothing, and their hands and faces, were stains ; and round about their bodies, and in the deep footmarks of the trampled space, stood little pools and runlets of some dark fluid that resembled the ooze which fills the hoof-prints of cattle at their drinking places in marshy ground.

The sun had not fully mastered the situation, nor quite dispelled the reluctant gloom—which slipped from shelter to shelter, hovering behind walls and lurking in retired corners, until spied out and dissipated by some ray of light detached for that purpose from the main body—when a tent at some distance from the Bouser establishment was thrown open, and two citizens, who had apparently not poured excessive libations the previous evening, issued forth. These two, after yawning, stretching, and rubbing their eyes, turned, as by a common impulse, towards the Bouser saloon, and merely glancing at the three still forms in the roadway as they passed, entered, loudly calling for the host. To them presently arrived a shock-headed, black moustached, heavy-jowled man, who, without further words. and as though any question concerning their errand was entirely superfluous, took down from a shelf a bottle and glasses, and pouring a few drops of bitters into the tumblers, rested his hands on the board which served as a counter, and waited until they had drank. Each of the citizens poured himself a lusty bumper; each tossed it off as if the loss of a single moment might be fatal; and each, as he set down his glass, sighed deeply, as expressing inward satisfaction and substantial refreshment. This ceremony performed, and the acolyte rewarded, the taller of the two citizens, a brawny, deep-chested, heavy-bearded man, addressing the bar-keeper, remarked in a chatty way:

"Well; so there were three handed in their checks last night, eh?"

"Guess there was four," was the reply, the speaker meanwhile mixing (more carefully than for his customers) *his* morning cocktail.

"There's only three outside, any way," struck in the second citizen—a wiry, yellow, unwholesome-looking man, with a straw-colored goatee.

"T'other must ha' crawled into the sage, then," said Mr. Bouser; "but there was four shot, I'll take my oath!"

"Well," observed the tall citizen, after a pause, "I s'pose you'll have the stiffs hauled out afore breakfast? It's Sunday, and more o' the boys 'll be in from the road. They aint particular, I know, but, there's some as *does* object to seein' so many lyin' around."

At this, Mr. Bouser's brows descended, and he gruffly intimated that "twarn't no business o' his any how. Them as did the shootin' oughter do the buryin'! They was allers playin' off onto him some such games, and he warn't agoin' to stand it."

To this the wiry man quietly rejoined, that the "stiffs" were right in front of Mr. Bouser's own door, and might, perhaps, interfere with his business. The force of this argument being acknowledged with a snarl, the two citizens retired, and took a stroll up the street, which by this time was beginning to look more lively.

At intervals of a few minutes a tent door here and there would be flung apart, and a citizen would emerge. Some looked sleepy, some looked boozy, some looked sulky, some looked fierce, but none looked as though the light of the blessed sun was welcome to them, the pure, sweet air of the mountains refreshing, or the advent of another day productive of new hopes of any kind. In the course of an hour, Kill-me-Quick was pretty thoroughly awake, and at the rear of two or three larger shanties fires were burning briskly, preparing breakfast for the boarders—for those places aspired to the position of restaurants. Some few citizens went to the trouble of washing their faces in the little stream that flowed below the camp, but by far the majority preferred a stiff cocktail. As these assembled at Mr. Richard Bouser's bar, they naturally formed groups, and began to discuss the events of the evening before with much gusto, individuals occasionally stepping into the roadway to illustrate, with abundant gesture, supported by equally abundant oaths, the positions of the belligerents in the principal and most deadly broil.

The discussions often waxed warm, and on one occasion a citizen with one eye (the other having been lost in a slight difficulty) gave the lie so sharply to another citizen with half a nose, that the bystanders stepped back instinctively, as preparing to shun the shots which all supposed must follow. But whether it was that the Bouser cocktails were not up to fighting pitch, or that the presence of the three recumbent figures operated in some way as a deterrent, certain it is that no fight followed; and, perhaps for similar reasons, the crowd did not resent the disappointment of its expectations. Not that there was any reverence expressed for the dead. By no means. For instance, when a citizen of a suspiciously close-cropped and bullet-headed aspect fell into a dispute with a red-bearded and cross-eyed comrade as to the number of shots fired into one of the recumbent figures, the red-bearded one strode coolly to the corpse, turned it over with his foot, stooped, tore off the garments so as to expose the wounded side, and having gained his point, let the body drop again, not even troubling himself to replace the disturbed clothing. Death had no terrors, could claim no privileges, among the citizens of Kill-me-Quick.

For some time the discussion proceeded, now waxing warm, now fading in interest, until one individual, whose sense of propriety was more fastidious than his neighbors', remarked that "Bouser ought to move them things"—indicating the three bodies by a jerk of his thumb over the shoulder; and adding, that—"the gals 'd be out putty soon, and mightn't like it."

The observation struck a chord of common sympathy, evidently originating in the connection of "them gals" with the subject, and Mr. Bouser being expostulated with in a way more vigorous than polite, made a virtue of necessity, and asking them to drink with him, further begged them to take the bestowal of the "stiffs" off his hands. This was throwing himself upon their generosity, in a manner, and they at once agreed. Seeing that the obsequies of the deceased consisted merely in carrying them by the head and heels beyond the limits of the camp, and there throwing them down among the sage brush, the task could scarcely be regarded as an onerous one; and, as on returning Mr. Bouser was compelled to stand treat again, it may be said to have been amply remunerated. As for sanitary considerations respecting the burial of the dead, Kill-me-Quick entertained none. Its mission was accomplished, as its name implied, when the separation of soul from body was consummated. Beyond that it had no ideas; and as the citizens of Kill-me-Quick would very probably be the citizens of Deadfall, or Last Chance, or some other camp, within a week, this obliv-

iousness to the laws of hygiene was, after all, more apparent
than real.

And there was another reason for this neglect of the dead.
Kill-me-Quick was in a terrible hurry. It was always striving
to get ahead of Time. Its mission was to make money, and
that by the quickest possible road; and as the shortest roads
are in this regard the roughest and most dangerous, so Kill-me-
Quick went into the pursuit of riches, carrying its life in its
hand, or, to speak more correctly, balancing its life like that
metaphorical chip on its shoulder, to be knocked off or not, as
the fancy of the first fellow ruffian that came along might dic-
tate. To say that human life was held cheap at Kill-me-Quick
would convey no idea of the truth. It was simply a drug in the
market. A day or two before the time of this history, a gam-
bler named Phil. Batcher, who had been on a prolonged spree,
sobered up to a realization of the fact that he had played away
all his money, and nearly all his partner's. who happened to be
absent. On this discovery he took what was left, repaired to
the scene of his losses, challenged the winner to another game
of poker, and lost his last dollar. Then he threw down the
cards, rose, and in a calm voice requested his late antagonist to
shoot him. To this the other demurred, as lacking a motive for
shooting. Mr. Batcher, seeing his hesitancy, and divining the
cause, upon this drew his pistol and swore he would shoot the
other if the other refused to shoot him. This settled the question. His opponent proposed that he should step to the limits
of the camp, so as to save trouble, and this being done, shot
him neatly through the head, he standing with folded arms to
receive the bullet. This affair served as a whet to breakfast
next morning, but long before noon it had ceased to be spoken
of.

Of course it was not to be expected that Kill-me-Quick, being
thus indifferent about its own life, should care much for the lives
of other people. It needed very little provocation to produce
pistols and knives, and the way in which the former were used
was very reckless. As a matter of fact, out of every five men
killed, two, on an average, were outsiders, who were unfor-
tunate enough to be in the neighborhood when a quarrel oc-

curred; and it was this uncertainty of aim which in a measure accounted for the survival of so many desperadoes of the most truculent kind. For, to say the truth, the citizens of Kill-me-Quick were about as bad as bad could be. Gathered up from the foulest dens of New York, Philadelphia, Baltimore, New Orleans, Chicago, and other centers of commingled civilization and barbarity, and plentifully besprinkled with that peculiar class of frontier ruffians who have added all the ferocity and cunning of the Indian to all the worst vices of the lowest classes of white men; assembled there, on the westernmost point of the advancing Pacific Railroad, for no other objects than robbery, swindling and plunder; inured to crime—the blackest and most infamous conceivable; as ready to cut each other's throats as the throats of the unwary travelers who might fall into their hands; gamblers, thieves, murderers, escaped convicts, cattle stealers, forgers, it would have been perhaps impossible to find, on all the continent of America, an assemblage of human beings more uniformly, desperately, irreclaimably wicked than the citizens of Kill-me-Quick.

And yet they were mostly deserving of study, too, for they in a measure held high degrees in crime. Scarce one among them but possessed a history of no mean interest. Scarce one but had passed some thrilling scenes, some hair-breadth escapes. I do not say that they were a *better* class than the sneak thief or the pick pocket of city life belong to, but they were certainly a *different* class. Any one of them would have killed a man for a fancied insult, or to obtain a few ounces of gold, or for mere pique. And any one of them would have flung his last dollar to a starving wretch, if the whim took him. It was light come, light go, no doubt. Little enough of true generosity, or indeed of any sentiment at all, among them. A set of men who never enjoyed themselves; whose revels were ferocious and terrifying, and never genial and festive; who could not utter a ringing, happy laugh, but when their dull sense of humor was touched gave vent to a sound that was more like a yell than a laugh—more indicative of pain than pleasure. They were men whose speech was habitually awfully profane; who never exhibited any originality save in coining new oaths; who were accustomed to employ the most terrific adjurations in their ordinary conversation, just as they employed the most deadly weapons in their ordinary business, and who seemed to be quite unconscious of any peculiarity in either respect.

Such were the male citizens of Kill-me-Quick, in so far as the traits held in common extended. Each one among them, of course, differed from his fellow in his inner life, and in the turn of his character, but these peculiarities were typical of the class. Such were the male citizens. What were the females like? In such a place, what could they be? Ah, you who reverence pure womanhood, who recognize in it the type and the full expression of the Divinity, after the likeness of which mankind was formed, turn your sad eyes away from these fallen Daughters of Light; believe, if you will, that the picture is exaggerated and untrue, rather than surrender your ideal or lose your ennobling faith. Not wholly void as yet of outward grace of form or figure; not wholly lacking, yet, in the witchery of feminine ways; not quite gone, yet, the power of the flashing eyes. But for all these, and more than ever because of these remnants of the past—differing from, separated from, other than, all women else.

Women who fall, fall farther than, and yet not so hopelessly as, men. There are men so saturated with evil, that could you peel them as one peels an onion, the last innermost layer would be reached and thrown away without discovering one single grain of good. There are no such women. The woman who falls presents a more callous exterior, *is* outwardly harder, plunges more desperately and recklessly into fresh crimes, pursues her downward path with a more entire abandon, and a more ostentatious rejection of every proffer of rescue. But for all this there burns longer and warmer in her heart the spark of love lit up in the beginning; and pile the ashes mountains high upon that spark, it remains unquenched and unquenchable.

Kill-me-Quick was a desperately wicked place. If a second Abraham had renewed for its people the plea which failed when put up for the Cities of the Plain, I fear the same rule would have excluded hope. But if by any chance enough of goodness had been found to fulfil the condition, I know full well that in the breast of one of these outcasts that remnant of purity could alone have been discovered. Not goodness such as the world would acknowledge, perhaps; not goodness such as would be regarded sufficient for salvation by Society; but yet so much of purity and heaven-born tenderness as exists in a love stronger than cruelty, stronger than outrage, stronger than shame, stronger than death itself. Such virtue as lives in a love so self-forgetful as to cling, with the grasp of a despairing soul, around the image of the unworthy wretch who betrays the heart that trusts him.

No thoughts of this kind, however, disturbed the serenity of the traveler who, about noon on the Sunday in question, rode into the main street of Kill-me-Quick, and dismounted in front of the tent where Mr. Richard Bouser was by this time dispensing liquid refreshments at a lively rate, not only to the crowd that hummed and buzzed in and out of the doorway, like truculent blue bottles, but to the crowd that, divided into knots, was deeply absorbed in the delights of poker and seven-up, at the rear of the establishment.

The new arrival was in more respects than one worth looking at. In the first place, he looked so much more like an honest man than any of the usual frequenters of the camp; in the second place, he was much more comely than the average of the citizens of Kill-me-Quick—the most of whom, in addition to the trade marks which Dame Nature sets upon her inferior productions, carried about them such mementos of brawls and affrays as imparted an additionally sinister aspect to their countenances. The stranger was apparently thirty years of age, of medium hight, broad shoulders, and powerfully built, possessing an open and cheerful face, lighted by two dark blue eyes, and finished off by a luxuriant brown beard. He was clothed plainly in a suit of coarse homespun, and wore long, travel-stained boots. As he sprang from the saddle and threw the reins on the neck of his Indian pony—a rough but serviceable little beast—he encountered a sharp scrutiny from a dozen pair of eyes, belonging to as many citizens, who were lounging about the saloon. Kill-me-Quick was always very prompt in deciding the status of new comers, and in determining the line of conduct to be adopted concerning them. In the present instance, Kill-me-Quick summed up the stranger about as follows: "A green hand. Probably a Mormon elder. May have greenbacks. Our meat." And having thus concluded, a deputation was, by pantomime and exchange of rapid glances rather than by words, appointed to wait upon the new arrival.

The stranger, whom for the present we will designate according to the conclusions of Kill-me-Quick, as the Green Hand, strode into the saloon, flinging a general "good day, boys!" to right and left as he entered. Approaching the counter, he called for a drink, and as at this moment two citizens, detaching themselves from the crowd, advanced a step or two and directed an inquiring look at him, he invited them to join him.

The two citizens thus invited were the two who have been already introduced while taking their morning cocktail. The taller was named Jack Belto, commonly called "Slaughterhouse Jack," from a way he had of felling his opponents. The wiry, yellow-faced man, was Amasa Cobbins, *alias* "Knifey," so called from his preference for the invention of Colonel Bowie over the invention of Colonel Colt.

Cheerfully accepting the invitation of the Green Hand, these gentlemen stepped forward, and filling their glasses, drained them to the brief but expressive toast, "here's luck."

Naturally a conversation followed, in the course of which they learned that the Green Hand (who must have been very green, judging from the openness with which he discussed his affairs) was a Mormon trader from Salt Lake City, on his way to California to make purchases for his store. He was so frank and guileless that his new companions found no difficulty in ascertaining that he carried with him a considerable sum of money, but perhaps this absence of suspicion was caused by the belief he seemed to entertain that Kill-me-Quick was a construction camp belonging to the railroad. Messrs. Belto and Cobbins took care not to undeceive him in this respect, and presently proposed that he should take a stroll, after watering his horse, as he would have plenty of time to reach the advance camp of the Central Pacific Railroad before dark. Nothing loth, he assented, and the three stepped into the street.

By this time Kill-me-Quick was wide awake, and attending to its interests. Many railroad men were already in camp, and more were dropping in, by twos and threes. Pretty hard customers, generally, were these same railroad men; men who had been scraped up here and there along the line of the road, as it progressed westward, and many of whom had good reasons for desiring to be beyond the reach of civilization for a time. It is unnecessary to state that the terrors of the law fell far short of the region in which Kill-me-Quick was situated, and that Police Courts and Sheriffs were unknown there. Every man was a law to himself, and as the only law recognized was that of self-interest, the result was, as has been shown, peculiar. The chief business of Kill-me-Quick was gambling, and this business was pursued fiercely. Faro, monte, poker, seven-up, and a dozen other games, were in full blast, in as many tents and shanties, as the Green Hand and his escort strolled through the camp. Some few men were washing a shirt or so in the brook; others were cleaning and reloading their weapons. At the door of a tent which stood a little apart from the rest, two girls were seated. They were gaudily, though not richly dressed. Their eyes were bright, though not with health. Their cheeks were wan and hollow, but their looks were hard and brazen, and defiant and reckless. They stared at the Green Hand as he passed, and seemed about to address him, but a motion of the hand from Belto checked them, and after whispering together they laughed loudly and re-entered the tent.

The trio sauntered through the camp, and back to the saloon, the Green Hand all the time talking freely, and his companions doing their best to adapt themselves to his mood. Another drink was taken, and then Cobbins, after a glance at his comrade, proposed a game of cards to pass the time until dinner was ready. The stranger, however, did not care to play just then—would rather talk, in fact—so without pressing him further, the two indulged his humor, and chatted away pleasantly until the homely meal—for Kill-me-Quick was not great in the commissariat department—was ready. Then all three sat down, and presently the Green Hand, consulting an old-fashioned silver watch, announced his determination to proceed on his journey.

On hearing this Cobbins stepped for a moment behind him and telegraphed something to Belto, who responded by a cautious wink. A final drink was then proposed, and the three stepped up to the bar. Somehow or other Mr. Richard Bouser was rather longer than usual in preparing the cocktails, but at last they were set down. The two citizens seized their glasses and hastily raised them to their lips, at the same time wishing their friend a pleasant journey. He was about to follow their example, but suddenly lowered his hand, and uttering an exclamation of disgust, threw his cocktail on the ground. A glance passed between the confederates, and Belto asked what was the matter.

"There was a fly in the liquor," said the Green Hand, "and I never can stand them things."

"Mix another cocktail, Dick," said Cobbins, and see that there's no flies in it this time."

"But the stranger interrupted, saying, "Oh, never mind! I'll take mine straight rather than keep you waiting;" and did so. Whereupon Belto and Cobbins looked at each other again, and this time as though they had been baffled in something. But the next moment their faces brightened on hearing the stranger exclaim :

"Well, boys, I havn't had a game of cards for a long while, and though 'taint the thing for an elder, and on a Sunday, I guess I'll run the risk of sinning for once, and play you for the drinks."

So the matter was arranged, and Belto, Cobbins and the Green Hand sat down to play at a table improvised out of a flour barrel, in the back of a tent.

There never were three players whose luck and skill seemed more equally matched. The game was old sledge, and it was pleasant to note how each in turn won, and how cheerful and amiable the two representatives of Kill-me-Quick were. It was evident that they were impressed with the responsibility of their position, as hosts, and that all they desired was to give the stranger a favorable opinion of the camp. For an hour or so they played on innocently and quietly, the only noticeable fact during this period being that the Green Hand declined to take

the chances of any more flies in his liquor, and insisted on filling
a bottle for himself from the whisky barrel, "just for the fun of
the thing," as he remarked. But presently Mr. Belto began to
yawn and stretch himself, and on being interrogated as to the
cause of his apparent weariness, replied that he was tired of
"this no 'count kind o' play. There warnt 'nuff interest 'bout
the thing to suit *him*, nohow."

Mr. Cobbins, upon this, suggested that they should play
poker for small money stakes, and the stranger readily assent-
ing, Mr. Belto recovered his interest and the game proceeded.

The Green Hand was unquestionably a good player, but he
was no less unquestionably an unsuspicious player. His partners had made several little quiet experiments during the first
hour, and the result was a beaming conviction that their task
would be an easy one, and that all that was necessary was
caution and moderation.

So the game went on all the afternoon, and when the men
rose at dark to get their supper and stretch their legs, the
Green Hand was a hundred dollars or so ahead, and things had
become so interesting that there was no danger of his desiring
to quit play. They had their supper, and a smoke, and then retired as before to the rear of the tent, the Green Hand having
previously looked after his horse and tied him in a secure place.
It was tolerably clear that he would not proceed on his journey
that night. Perhaps Kill-me-Quick may have doubted whether
his journey's end was not almost reached already.

And the game went on. Gradually the stakes were raised,
and gradually the run of luck began to desert the Green Hand,
and to hover between Messrs. Belto and Cobbins. Kill-me-
Quick, as the evening wore on, seemed to become much interested in the play, and quite a crowd collected about the trio,
some lounging against the sides of the shanty, some standing
with their hands in their pockets, pondering the cards, others
smoking or chewing; and yet others flitting restlessly about,
hovering first over one player and then another, and advancing
and retreating softly, as though performing some peculiar kind
of dance. Mr. Bouser had done honor to the occasion (for the
report had gone round that Belto and Cobbins had a big thing

on hand) by lighting a coal-oil lamp, which was swung from the canvas roof by a cord. It was the only coal-oil lamp in the place, and he was consequently not a little proud of it.

So the game went on. The stranger appeared to be perfectly self-possessed, never rated his luck, never insinuated anything about his opponents' play, never got flushed or flurried, and never noticed the crowding of the interested citizens about him. He always responded promptly to any challenge, and bet not only freely but wildly. By half-past eight o'clock he had lost five hundred dollars. At ten he was a thousand dollars poorer. Belto and Cobbins were beginning to lose their heads with the consciousness of victory, and more than once cheated so openly and clumsily that the stranger could hardly have failed to detect them, had he not been so *very* green. The bystanders from time to time retired to compare opinions and refresh themselves, and the whispered comments were by no means flattering to the intellectual powers of the Green Hand.

So the game went on. The Green Hand was now losing " every pop," as Mr. Bouser phrased it, but bore his losses with equanimity. At last, however, while Mr. Cobbins was dealing a fresh pack, he rose, turned the box he was seated on, gravely explained " for luck," and re-seated himself. This gamblers' superstition was so well known and so common, that the act would have excited no remark from any one there, but for this fact—that immediately thereafter the luck *did* begin to change. It was not that the stranger altered his style of play, but that somehow, although his opponents tried all their tricks, his cards would come out best. The fact began to dawn upon them after a few minutes that the Green Hand was actually cheating *them*. Amazing and incomprehensible as it might be, yet so it was. Of that there could be no question, and for this reason, that no man who played fairly *could* win from Messrs. Belto and Cobbins. They employed freely all the customary frauds. They had the deck in the breast, and the deck in the sleeve, and the cards were marked, and Belto had a large hand—and, in short, a fair and square player had simply no chance at all with them.

But the game went on. And if Belto and Cobbins were

amazed at the change in their luck, the citizens of Kill-me-Quick were more than amazed; they were thunderstruck. It is true that none of them entertained serious doubts of the final issue, knowing that the game could be terminated at any moment by getting up a row and shooting the stranger. But there was a curious kind of artistic feeling about the affair. They had pitted their most expert swindlers against this fellow, and he was beating them at their own game. To kill him would settle the question of the ownership of the money, but it would leave unsettled the other question of which was the best and most skillful cheater; and this was of some importance. Kill-me-Quick, thus thinking, and watching the game without being able to detect the stranger's mode of working, became nervous and irritable, and a few of the more impatient spirits, unable longer to control their mortification, went outside, got up a a fight, and carved a railroad contractor, whose ill luck had brought him into the neighborhood, into small pieces.

In the meantime, the game went on. At one A. M. the Green Hand had not only won back his money, but had secured six hundred dollars of his opponents' funds. At this time the latter exchanged glances, and each saw that the other had determined to end the matter speedily. They went on playing, however, awaiting a favorable opportunity, and at half-past one o'clock the stranger had raked in one thousand dollars in greenbacks, and continued to produce the most astonishing hands. Just at this time another fight occurred outside, and the crowd rushed out to witness or take part in it, as fancy might suggest. A bet had been made, called and doubled, and Belto threw down four aces.

The stranger quietly produced *five* aces.

Both partners dropped their cards, and gazed open-mouthed at the audacity of this proceeding, and then Belto, with an air of virtuous indignation, observed:

"Stranger, I reckon you take us for suckers?"

"Guess not!" was the cool reply. "Guess I take you for card sharps."

It was apparent that the crisis had come.

Cobbins rose. "Stranger," he observed, at the same time reaching to grasp the money on the table, "You're a —— —— swindler."

In an instant, before the words were out of his mouth—before his hand was within six inches of the money—it was whipped from the table by the Green Hand, who at the same moment sprang to his feet. Belto's hand was already on his pistol, and Cobbins' knife was half out of its sheath, when a quick gleam of steel flashed in the air above them, the lamp fell crashing between them and their intended victim; there was an explosion, and a sheet of flame leaped up in their faces and drove them back. Belto fired his pistol at random, and Cobbins, dazzled for the moment, made a dash for the door to intercept the stranger. The burning oil rapidly fired the rough boards and canvas of the tent, and all was confusion, cursing, shouting, smoke and glare. The crowd rushed back from the street to find Mr. Bouser's establishment burning furiously, and Belto and Cobbins raging like fiends about the doorway. But the Green hand had availed himself of that moment of surprise and confusion caused by the fall of the lamp, and before his enemies could satisfy themselves that he had escaped from the tent, he had mounted, and was riding furiously over the hills. The instant his escape was discovered, a dozen men threw themselves on horseback and started in pursuit. For half an hour dropping rifle and pistol shots were heard, and then the baffled pursuers rode slowly back, while on a distant eminence a man stood, holding his horse's bridle over his arm, and smilingly surveying a blaze that made the dark sky lurid above the valley, and betokened the destruction of the lively camp of Kill-me-Quick.

CHAPTER II.

ON THE DOWN GRADE.

It is to be regretted, on ethical grounds, that the fire which speedily consumed the tents and shanties of Kill-me-Quick did not involve the people of the place; but as such an event would have rendered the continuation of this history impossible, perhaps all was for the best. Messrs. Belto and Cobbins were last seen raging and foaming over the escape of their victim (who by common consent ceased from that time to be alluded to as the Green Hand, and was thereafter designated as " that durn' skunk "). These gentlemen were very angry, not only with the fugitive, who had got away with their funds, but with themselves, each other, and all Kill-me-Quick. After the fire had burned out, which was not until the last combustible thing within its scope was consumed, the people of the late camp of Kill-me-Quick gathered morosely about the embers, and arranged their plans for the future. The burning of the tents did not trouble them much, as they possessed little destructible property, Bouser being perhaps the only one who sustained anything like a serious loss. So, after cursing the "durn' skunk" to their heart's content, and making parties to go this way and that on the morrow, to try their fortune anew at Dead Fall, or Corinne, or some other new place on the line of the railroad, the choicer spirits turned their attention to chaffing Belto and Cobbins, who, being very sore and mortified, were in a fit state to be baited. The *badinage* indulged in was of a kind not to be conveyed by any recognized words in the English language, and it would therefore be impossible to reproduce even a specimen of the conversation that ensued. It was, however, intended to convey that the community regarded the conduct of Messrs. Belto and Cobbins most unfavorably ; that they had lost caste with their friends ; that they need never again set themselves up as gamblers and murderers of talent and parts ; that they had brought shame and humiliation upon Kill-me-Quick, and had abused the confidence heretofore reposed in them.

The partners having borne these reproaches for some time with a kind of professional stoicism, though inwardly chafing, at length came to the conclusion that it was time to put an end to it, and proceeded to wind up the business characteristically. They were at the moment in the center of a circle, the members composing which were all equally guilty of chaffing them. There being therefore no room for choice, Mr. Belto, raising his voice, though without passion, expressed an opinion that the

2

whole gathering were closely allied to the canine race, and des-
tined to eternal punishment.   Having uttered this sentiment,
he quickly drew his revolver, singled out his man, and shot him
in his tracks, while at the same moment Mr. Cobbins made
effective play with his knife.   The crowd instinctively fell back
when the firing commenced, and the two partners at once broke
out of the circle and ran for their horses.   In another minute
the majority had recovered from their confusion and followed
them, keeping up a rapid but ineffectual fusillade.   The fugitives gained the saddle, and knowing the country something
better than their pursuers, succeeded in getting away, while the
latter returned to discuss this last incident, and finally rolled
themselves in their blankets and went to sleep with a general
impression that the evening had turned out pretty lively,
after all.

In the meantime, the fugitives were discussing the future as
they rode, and having concluded that there was not much in
the prospect westward, unless they went on to California (for
which they were not yet prepared), determined to go back on
the line of the railroad as far as Echo, and " make a raise" there
among the railroad laborers.   As, however, these laborers were
all armed, and accustomed to use their weapons on slight provocation, it was deemed prudent to guard against accidents, and
to that end it was arranged that Mr. Cobbins should go on to
Echo first, and on his arrival should make it his business to
gamble with the " boys " for their pistols, by securing which,
possibly unpleasant consequences might be averted.   The fact
that the railroad hands had not been paid for some weeks, and
were expecting money every day, favored this programme, having settled which, the partners divided the funds in hand and
separated, Belto agreeing to follow on the second day, when the
way would be prepared for their joint operations.

On the second day after these events, Mr. Cobbins alighted
from a construction train on which he had secured a passage,
and walked into the town of Echo, or Echo City, as it was
christened, in accordance with the prevailing custom to call
everything a city consisting of more than three buildings, belonging to more than two persons.

Echo City, at the period of our history, consisted of about fifty buildings, of wood, of wood and canvas, and of canvas alone. The permanent residents (the place was fully two months old) were all storekeepers and whisky dealers. The floating population consisted of railroad hands and gamblers, with a sprinkling of passengers. Situated at the base of a huge cliff, that towered some two hundred feet into the air above it, the dimensions of Echo City, never very imposing, were dwarfed still more by the contrast of its surroundings; and the traveler coming suddenly on the place was apt to imagine for a moment that the buildings were merely doll-houses, and not real dwellings and stores. There were, even at this early stage of the city's existence, two hotels, which had already established a smart rivalry. To say truth, there was not very much to choose between them, both being equally bad and equally dear. The accommodations were somewhat meager, being limited in the Walker House to an airy but low-roofed loft, immediately over the bar-room, and in the Echo Hotel to the interior of a barn which also served as a harness and lumber room, and was not wholly free from a suspicion of rats. The Walker House was perhaps most liberally patronized, for the reason that it possessed a billiard saloon; but as neither this nor the bar were ever closed, and as both apartments were filled day and night with a free-and-easy crowd, who alternated drinking and billiards with cursing and fighting; and as the planks which formed the floor of the loft and the bed of the lodgers were too thin to stop bullets, the attempt to seek rest in that quarter was open to the charge of being a pursuit of sleep under difficulties.

Mr. Walker, the proprietor of the house, was a little man, with a dry, thick head of sandy hair, which stood stiffly up, and which seemed to express the perpetual surprise its owner felt at being where he was. Mr. Walker was always in a hurry, though he never did anything. He knew nothing of the resources of his establishment, and was completely controlled by a keen, dark-whiskered man who acted as his clerk, and who divided his time between registering the names of the guests, and making calculations as to the extreme possible limit their bills could be stretched to.

The guests of the Walker House were mostly of that class who carry their own blankets with them, and whose night toilet is made by pulling off their boots, which then do duty as a pillow. There were a good many oily and grimy firemen, who wiped their faces with bunches of cotton waste; grave looking but rough spoken engineers, who had acquired an expression of power and responsibility through their long wrestlings with the Spirit of Steam; hardy, foul-mouthed, ruffianly railroad hands; equally hardy, less foul-mouthed and more decent mechanics, carpenters, bridge builders, blacksmiths, track layers, and a dozen other varieties of the genus railroad man. All these and such as these, besprinkled with a dozen or two of sharpers and moral agriculturists, kept Echo City lively enough, and occasionally the scene was varied by the appearance of a score of passengers, who gazed wildly about them, ordered drinks at the bar hurriedly, drank them hesitatingly, and paying for them reluctantly, walked off shudderingly, wiping their lips doubtingly, as though half expecting that the fiery stuff would burn holes in the fabric.

The stores at Echo were not numerous, but omniverous. All of them professed to keep everything, and the stocks generally included most necessaries, from a suit of clothes to a tin dipper. The storekeepers were bustling men, always on the lookout for good speculations, and always putting up new frame buildings. Echo was, in fact, building all the time, and the clang of hammers and the grating of saws divided the honors with the scream of locomotive whistles, the melancholy sound of locomotive bells, and the rumble of approaching and departing trains.

To such a scene was Mr. Cobbins introduced, though not for the first time. In truth, this gentleman looked upon railroad towns as the normal condition of things. He had spent some years in following the dregs of civilization as they were pushed westward, and his general impressions bore a curiously grotesque resemblance to the traditionally reported opinions of Colonel Boone, the famous pioneer. Like that redoubtable personage, Mr. Cobbins entertained an aversion to crowded cities, though certainly from different motives. The "clearings" avoided by him were the clearings made by the establishment of law and order.

He regarded Courts, Sheriffs and jails as products of an effete
civilization, and in his gloomier moments was wont to take a
depressing view of the condition of the age, observing at such
times that "There was mighty little show nowadays for a man to
get a square living, wot with them d—d newspapers and new-
fangled ideas 'bout sportin' caracters." But it was seldom that he
gave way to such reflections, being on the whole inclined to be
extremely practical, and acting generally upon the principle
that "sufficient for the day is the evil thereof," a maxim applied
by him in a manner that would perhaps have startled the orthodox.

In the present instance he had no time for vain imaginings.
His work was cut out for him, and he proceeded to set about it
with characteristic energy and shrewdness. There were many
track-layers at Echo just then, for as the line was approaching
completion some hundreds had been sent back from the front,
and were waiting to be paid off before proceeding further east-
ward. These men were mostly armed, and being a desperate
class generally, it was rather a hazardous undertaking to fleece
them. One or two of Mr. Cobbins' particular friends had found
this out to their cost, and not being quick enough in taking a
hint had closed their careers at the end of a rope, hastily adjusted
to the nearest tree. Bearing these incidents in mind, our ad-
venturer determined to guard against one class of accidents as
much as possible by securing all the weapons of his intended
victims; and as the men were speedily going back to civilization, and a careless set, he found little difficulty in carrying out
his plans and winning their pistols from them. He looked upon
this as time and money well bestowed, even if he lost, because
he was confident that when his partner arrived they would win
back every dollar so expended.

The headquarters of Mr. Cobbins were at the Walker House,
where he managed to secure a nice little side room off the bar
for the operations of the morrow. In the meantime, having
filled his portmanteau with pistols, he devoted the remainder of
the day to making himself agreeable, which he did by standing
treat to all hands, by playing billiards and losing, and by initia-
ting half a dozen of the men from whom he feared trouble most

into the mysteries of some gambling fraud, which seemed easy enough when shown, but which the student could never after perform so as to deceive anybody. So the time passed cheerfully at Echo, and though the evening was noisy and slightly "lively," the exuberance of spirits noticeable at Kill-me-Quick was chastened here by the knowledge that a set of men who called themselves Mormon police were in charge of the town, and (notwithstanding the peculiar character of their creed) were by no means the kind to be trifled with.

On the morrow Mr. Belto appeared, urbane, genial and sprightly, and his partner having circulated the announcement that they proposed to start a "little game" at the Walker House, and the paymaster's car having also arrived, a brisk business was speedily commenced. Mr. Cobbins' favorite game was three-card monte—an amusement which has the advantage of being perfectly safe (for the dealer), as he cannot by any possibility lose a bet unless he makes a mistake and deals fairly—an error never to my knowledge committed by a professional. On this occasion, however, faro was introduced, and Mr. Belto had an opportunity of exhibiting his thorough acquaintance with the ingenious mechanism of a little silver box, so deftly fitted with delicate springs as to render the game *almost* as safe a one as three-card monte.

The partners played with their victims skillfully. Whenever they got a suspicious customer they allowed him to win, but gradually squeezed him out of the game. Whenever they got an impetuous customer they gave plenty of line, and at length landed him neatly, high and dry. All day long there was a steady stream of men flowing towards the paymaster's car, and another stream flowing from the paymaster's car to the little side room in the Walker House. The game was very successful, and consequently as evening approached the knots of discontented, impoverished players who collected outside began to increase rapidly. Mr. Cobbins, sallying out to reconnoiter, during a temporary lull, did not like the aspect of affairs. He observed that there was a disposition among the knots to merge into a crowd, that there was a disposition among the grumbling members of the knots to raise their voices and speak angrily and loudly, and that there was a disposition to join in a chorus, among the words of which (all very vigorous) the expressions "hogging game," "d—d thieves," "lynch 'em," etc., were plainly distinguishable.

Returning to the little side room he conveyed, in a whispered communication, the results of his reconnoissance to Mr. Belto, and the latter gentleman, though outwardly calm, evidently shared in the uneasiness so created. He was loth to leave the harvest partly ungathered, however, and pressed for a little more time. Mr. Cobbins shook his head, and at that moment a loud muttering sound caught their ears. It was suc. ceeded by a stern cry, embodying the sentiments expressed in the chorus referred to previously, and it settled the question. Rapidly securing about their persons the fruits of the day's enterprise, the worthy pair slipped quietly out at the back door, hoping to get on board a train which they knew was about to start for the front. In order to reach the railroad, however, they had to pass the main street, and though they made a long detour, and came out at the lower end of the town, near the telegraph office, they failed to elude their indignant victims. It seems that Mr. Walker, fearful that revenge would be taken on his establishment, had pointed out to the angry men the course taken by the gamblers, and the result was that when they emerged from the rear of the houses they found themselves within fifty feet of a furious mob, advancing with cries of rage and fearful threats and execrations, toward them.

Another glance showed them that the train on which they had relied was already moving out of the station, and they saw at once that if they could succeed in reaching the cars they were saved—and lost if they failed. It is surprising how fast men not otherwise fitted for or trained to such exercises will run, with a metaphorical halter about their necks. Messrs. Belto and Cobbins, on this occasion, rivaled the famous Deerfoot, and as their efforts were stimulated by yells, curses, and occasional pistol shots (for they had not succeeded in securing *all* the weapons), there was no chance for any relaxation of their speed. Indeed, it was a hot chase. More than once the gamblers thought it was a vain chase. But fortune favors the bold, and they reached the cars and sprang upon them just as the train was getting well under way. The crowd behind hooted and yelled, and flung stones, and continued to run forward· But the chase was ended, to all intents and purposes, and the baffled laborers were compelled to return, solacing themselves with the reflection that if ever they got Messrs. Belto and Cobbins in their hands again—well, they would see.

Some minutes passed before the panting gamblers had recovered sufficiently to look about them, but when they did they found themselves on one of the rear trucks of a train loaded with wooden ties, and having a caboose behind the engine. As this car seemed to present better prospects of comfort than the open truck on which they were standing they determined to make their way to it, and forthwith proceeded to clamber over the ties. They had reached within one car of the caboose when its door was opened and a man appeared on the platform and looked toward them.

The recognition was instantaneous and mutual. It was the Green Hand—the "durn skunk"—who had burned Kill-me-Quick and secured their money. .

Each of the three uttered an exclamation. The stranger's was one of surprise; Mr. Belto's was one of fierce hatred and anger, and Mr. Cobbins' was one of ominous determination. The next instant the two partners were scrambling over the ties to get at their enemy.

He saw their movement, divined its intention, glanced behind and around him, then quickly stooped. Rising in a moment he coolly folded his arms and smiled in their faces as they descended upon the platform of the last car that interposed between them. Mr. Belto was about to spring across when Cobbins caught him by the arm and held him back, exclaiming: "Hold on ! The durn skunk's uncoupled the train !"

As he spoke, the engine, caboose, and one car of ties shot forward, relieved of the weight of the rear cars, and a space of a hundred yards was speedily placed between the gamblers and their enemy.

But the end was not yet. When the stranger uncoupled the train he did it as a desperate resort, and did not take into account his surroundings. On leaving Echo City the grade descends rapidly, after a short level, and for twenty miles the pitch is ninety feet to the mile. By uncoupling the train the engine was made the lighter portion, and the heavily loaded rear cars, descending unchecked, threatened ruin and destruction to all in front of them. The danger was imminent and deadly.

The conductor saw what had happened, though he did not know how it had occurred, and springing on to the engine caused the throttle valve to be thrown wide open, and every pound of steam put on.

The dusk of evening was settling over the scene as this fearful race began. The Weber river dashed and foamed beside the track, as though bent on outstripping the train. Mile after mile was passed, and still the terrible cars thundered in pursuit of the engine. The open country was left behind, and the roaring train dashed into the gloom of the Weber Canyon. High on either hand the gray walls of rock towered grandly, while the furious river, lashed and torn by great jagged rocks, and maddened with the torture, chafed, and foamed, and hurled itself forward with blind recklessness; now plunging downward into deep, dark gorges, from the recesses of which its hoarse voice resounded awfully; now emerging into the light, and pouring in one shining volume through some clearly, smoothly cut defile, only to be broken and rent into fragments again a few yards further on. The tall trees rustled and bent in the blast that, rising at set of sun, swept through the narrow canyon as through a mighty funnel, and shrieked and moaned far up among the bleak, scarred crags that crowned the summit of the ravine. The engine labored; the fires roared and glowed; the sweating fireman piled fuel in the furnace for dear life; the engineer, pale as death, but with steady hand and eye, eased the mighty machine, and oiled it here and there; the conductor stood upon the tender, his whole figure breathing the most intense excitement, his hand lifted as a signal to the engineer, his eyes bent upon the coming horror. And there, ever close and closer yet, rolled and thundered the pursuer, slowly but surely lessening the distance.

The stranger stood on the platform of the caboose. He was pale but collected, and there was a bitterness upon his lips that spoke almost of recklessness. He was gazing at the approaching cars, on which the two gamblers, now scared out of all thought of revenge, clung with desperate grip, as the trucks beneath them sprang along the track. Suddenly, as he gazed, a soft voice, trembling, asked :

" Oh, sir, what is all this ? Why are we going so fast ? Is there any danger ? "

He started and turned to look at his questioner, a young girl, with great blue eyes, pure complexion, sweet mouth and abundant brown hair—a girl whose appearance would have arrested attention anywhere. Quietly dressed, in a dark, plain traveling suit; easy of carriage ; soft of voice ; gentle and well-bred of manner. The stranger regarded her at first with surprise, then with curiosity, then with a mingled expression of interest and distress.

" Madam," he at length replied, "it would be folly to deny that we are in danger—great danger. Those cars you see behind us have been detached from the engine, and unless we can keep ahead of them until we reach the next station they will run into and wreck us. But may I ask how you came to be here. I thought there were no other passengers than myself on board !"

The girl had become very pale while he was speaking, but now she put both her hands on his arm, and said, simply : " Oh, sir, I am on my way to meet my lover. We were to have been married on my arrival in California. But now—" she replied with a frightened look at the cars thundering on behind, and burst into tears.

The stranger was touched and troubled. He led her back into the caboose, uttered such words of comfort as came to his lips, and begging her to keep a good heart, assured her he would return soon, and went out with a new thought and a new determination. Springing on the last car, and calling the conductor to aid him, he began throwing the ties off, in the track of the advancing trucks. Vain hope ! The swooping cars caught the heavy timbers and flung them bodily into the air on either side of the track, as the waves of ocean fling their spray aloft. The men redoubled their energies, and piled heap on heap of ties upon the track. The pursuer descended upon and scattered them as though they had been heaps of dry leaves.

And the night fell as the fearful race progressed. The last rays of the sun gilded the craggy peaks, and brought out in strong relief the feathery boughs of the tallest pines; then sank away, and the gloom deepened through the canyon. The river still raved and raged beside the track, but now its course could only be traced by the white flashing of its foam-capped rapids. The furious pace at which they were going was shown no less by the fiery stream that encircled the wheels of the pursuing cars, than by the keen, sweeping, steady blast that opposed them.

They rushed through a tunnel, plunging, as it seemed, head-long at the mountain wall, and entering a yawning chasm that suddenly appeared, with a wild scream, to dash out again into the free air, past where a knot of workmen had kindled a huge fire, and stood around it, grim and weird in the ruddy light. A shout arose from the assembled workmen, was wafted away into the night as they plunged desperately forward, and again all was darkness, save where two streams of fiery sparks revealed the position of the advancing cars.

The engineer had done all that was in his power. The engine was taxed to its utmost fraction of endurance. Every available thing had been thrown upon the track, and every effort had failed. There was not fifty yards between them and a frightful death, and they know it. When all that could be had been done the stranger returned to the caboose and found the young girl—her name she said was Mary Sheldon—praying, and crying softly. She was very frightened, but it was evident that her thoughts were filled with distress, not on her own account, but because of the dear one who was about to lose her. In her simple, pure heart, she felt that death could bring no harm to her; but how would he live without her? So she cried softly, and thought very tenderly of her absent lover, praying more for him than for herself. And the stranger, noting her mood with quick observance, began to admire the girl, but in a way that he was not conscious of having admired any woman before. He tried to say something cheering to her, but there was not much to be said, and he soon realized that, and was silent—which was the best course that he could have taken.

And now there was a wild shout from the conductor, and the engineer's whistle was blown shrilly. He sprang into the open air and saw that a catastrophe was at hand.

Right in front of them was a bridge over a mountain torrent, and they were sweeping down upon it with the speed of the wind. But on the timbers of the bridge, and in the center of the track, and all about the bridge, could be seen, by the light of great fires kindled on the banks, men waving lanterns wildly, and gesticulating with frantic energy. The bridge had given way, and was even then being repaired. The warning was too late. The throttle valve was wide open, the last pound of steam was on, the engine was throbbing all over with the terrific energy of its action, as they swept like a whirlwind upon the bridge, dashed by the upturned horrified faces of the workmen, and rushed upon their fate.

There was no time for thought or action of any kind. They felt the timbers tremble; they felt the bridge swaying; they heard it creak——and then they were past and over it, dashing along again upon the firm track, in safety.

As they cleared the bridge the pursuing cars thundered down upon it. They were half way across when the whole structure shook, swayed, reeled for a moment to and fro, and then sank, with a crash heard above the roar of the torrent, into the dark waters below.

CHAPTER III.

TWO KINDS OF LOVE.

The town of Ogden, at the period of this history, was a very quiet, sober, humdrum little place. The Gentiles had not then invaded Utah as they have since, and their presence at Ogden was so rare as to be a matter for gossip. Ogden was thoroughly orthodox, from a Mormon point of view; thoroughly peaceful; thoroughly stagnant. Its little main street boasted about half a dozen stores, which did a small business with the brothers and sisters in the neighborhood, and occasionally supplied an outfit for some farmer who drove into town in a wagon unique in pattern, drawn by horses unacquainted with the luxury of the currycomb. The principal building in the place was the Tithing House, which stood within high walls of adobe, and presented a somewhat imposing and official appearance. Nearly opposite to this institution was the only place of entertainment known to Ogden, and that there might be no cause cause for scandal, this hostelry was presided over by a Bishop. The traffic up to this time had been chiefly confined to the Saints themselves, and the approach of the great railroad from both sides had brought many strangers into the narrow Ogden focus, and was beginning to stir up the somewhat sleepy Mormons to an appreciation of the fact that there were a good many people in the world, outside of Utah.

Strangers coming into Ogden from East or West used to say that they could always distinguish a Mormon from a Gentile, and further alleged that the Saints were characterized by a peculiar slouching gait and downcast expression, suggestive of priestly tyranny, and domestic burdens exceeding those which fall to the lot of monogamic people. Whether there was any foundation in fact for this fancy, matters little, but certain it is that the Saints at Ogden (as elsewhere) were very quiet in their demeanor; that the women dressed with a plainness not far removed from abominable ugliness of costume; and that the stranger who permitted his eyes to rove in the direction of any of these sisters was tolerably sure to encounter the watchful, suspicious, or angry gaze, of some jealous Saint, before long.

Bishop North, who kept the hotel, was a fine looking, intelligent man, and had ten wives. How he managed to get on with them all, is more than I know; but I have a shrewd suspicion that he did not always succeed in maintaining that harmony which is indispensable to the comfort of the domestic hearth—or hearths. Thus, on one occasion, having recently

taken his tenth spouse, he became imprudently enamored of
that damsel, and for a time neglected the nine other ladies who
were supposed to share his affections.   In fact, being then engaged in filling a contract for grading on the line of the railroad, he took Mrs. Bishop North Number Ten to live with him
in camp, and kept her there many weeks.   The ire of the be-
reaved nine was thereby aroused, and there came a day when
it was necessary to dispatch a messenger post haste to the contractor's camp, with the startling intelligence that a mutiny had
broken out in the Bishop's family, and that his presence on the
spot was absolutely required.   He returned to Ogden, and found
matters wearing so serious an aspect that it took three days to
negotiate a peace, and even then a cessation of hostilities was
only secured by certain humiliating concessions.   The Bishop
was a man of strong mind, but it has been whispered that his
defeat on this occasion broke his spirit, and that he was never
the same afterwards.   Certain it is that within a year his place
was vacant, and ten inconsolable widows mourned their liege
lord.

But that melancholy event was yet in the womb of the future
when, as dusk was falling on a certain summer evening, a passing train loaded with rails and other road material, stopped in
front of the long lane that leads from the track into the town,
and two passengers descended.   They were of opposite sexes,
young, good-looking, and apparently well-to-do.   The girl was
Miss Mary Sheldon.   The man was the stranger, whom, since
she addressed him as Mr. Broome, may be designated hereafter
by that name—which was in fact his own.

They had been thrown very much together since their strange
meeting on the train, and the girl had grown upon him greatly.
There had been trouble in reaching Ogden, for as there were no
regular trains they were often compelled to wait for long hours
at unfrequented parts of the track, or pass time away on sidings;
and thus much opportunity for conversation had occurred.   He
had learned from her her little history.   How she had became
engaged to young John Rutter, who had gone to California and
purchased an interest in a quartz mine.   How he was so busy
that he could not come all the way to her Eastern home to fetch

his bride, but had written to her to come on to Ogden, and had bespoken for her the attention of some of his married friends who were about returning to the West: how these friends had been prevented from returning as contemplated, by illness; and how she had determined to make the journey alone rather than disappoint him.

She had not been so successful in unravelling the skein of her companion's story. He was reticent in regard to himself, and all she could gather was that he was born in the East some-where, had been travelling and wandering for many years, and did not seem to be at all certain as to his destination, or at all determined as to his business when he arrived there. For the rest, he was kind and thoughtful; always on the watch to secure her comfort and ease; respectful in his address; cheerful and agreeable in his conservation; and altogether a very pleasant companion. This was the impression Henry Broome had created in the mind of the fair young creature he had as it were taken in charge. She was so full of her lover that all other men had ceased to be interesting to her, and her love was so wholly centered on the absent, that she was far more genial and unembarrassed with her new friend than she could have been under other circumstances.

The impression *she* had made upon *him* was a strong one, and yet in no sense dangerous for either of them. He found in her a simple, pure-minded, innocent girl. One of those girls whose perfect innocence is so much surer a protection to them than that much-lauded attribute called knowledge of the world, could be. Her conversation cheered and refreshed him, because it took him out of the grooves he had been traversing so long, and because it showed a mind which only recognized goodness and truth, and thus tacitly flattered all with whom it came in contact. Henry Broome had been wild, nay, wicked. He had dissipated, he had gambled, he had consorted with more than doubtful characters. He had done a great many things which it is neither necessary nor profitable to recount here; and he was just in that condition of mind when a little thing would determine his future either way—for good or for evil.

Mary Sheldon was not the kind of girl he could have fallen

in love with. He was not yet sufficiently softened to think of anything of the kind, indeed, having passed his later years among scenes of lawlessness and rude energy that excited and amused, while unsettling, him. But he felt that he took great pleasure in this sweet little girl, and he also felt that the com. panionship was doing him good. It would be much harder for him to return to the old wild life after having met her, than he perhaps imagined at the time, although even then he found himself occasionally wondering whether after all there might not be real pleasure and content in the society to which she naturally belonged.

So they became very friendly, indeed much more so than is usually the case when people are thrown together by accident. They had passed through a great danger together, and that was one bond of sympathy. She had suffered him to read her heart, in the moment when she thought the end had come; and that was another bond of sympathy. And so it happened that they were very chatty and merry together as they walked up the long lane from the railway, and that Bishop North, seeing them so friendly and intimate, concluded at once, with the wisdom of a much-married man, that they were not man and wife, and showed them to separate apartments.

But though Bishop North's matrimonial experience directed him aright, the brothers and sisters who saw the pair approaching, and who immediately fell to speculating about them, as people do in small places when strangers arrive, speedily suspected, with that lack of charity which is so very reprehensible and so very human, that there must be something wrong about them. In the first place they were evidently Gentiles, and being Gentiles, it was of course the most natural thing in the world that they should be wicked. In the next place they were evidently not married; and the Saints and Saintesses somewhat inconsequently argued from this that they ought to be. In the third and last place they had taken separate apartments, and this was regarded as a clear proof that there *must* be something wrong about them. Had they been as bad as the good people of Ogden wished to believe them, and had they undertaken to play the role of man and wife, the probability is that they would have escaped calumny. But being virtuous, and acting as virtuous people do act, they were at once set down as deep, designing hypocrites, and abandoned characters. Of course the good people of Ogden were much to blame for their censoriousness, but it seems to me that Ogden is not the only place in the world where such a thing might have happened.

However, being in happy ignorance of what was passing in the minds of the townfolk, the travelers calmly established themselves in their new quarters and proceeded to prepare for supper. John Rutter had not yet arrived, and there was nothing to do but to wait for his appearance.

The table kept by Bishop North was by no means a luxurious one; but, though it had been much more plentifully spread, Mary Sheldon would scarcely have noticed the difference. Of course she had no appetite, and her companion was so occupied in watching her (which he did with an amused curiosity, as a naturalist might study the habits of some newly discovered animal), that he, too, ate very little. Indeed, they both rose quickly from the table and retired to the Bishop's parlor, which he had kindly placed at their disposal.

Mary was nervous and excited. Every footstep that sounded on the stairs brought a flush to her cheek and a light to her eye, and after several ineffectual attempts to start a conversation, Henry came to the conclusion that the scheme was impracticable, and, lapsing into silence, attempted to amuse himself with the only book in the room, which happened to be a Directory of Salt Lake City.

But, though Mary could not enter into a serious conversation, she was equally unable to keep quiet; and, after rising a dozen times to look out of the window, and glancing as often at her watch, and sighing, and fidgeting about the room, she began asking her companion questions, and forgetting his answers before he had finished them.

Presently, however, a diversion was effected by the appearance of the Bishop, who brought an offering of a wonderful home-made beverage which he called champagne, and which was solemnly drunk, with many expressions of delight and satisfaction, and much inward shuddering and mental disturbance.

3

After a few minutes the Bishop (who addressed Mary as Sister Sheldon, much to her astonishment and alarm, for she did not know but that this might constitute, in some mysterious way, a claim on her allegiance to the Mormon Church), rose and bowed himself out, and then, the ice being broken, the young couple chatted freely and comfortably about the manners and customs of the Saints. Of course Mary was curious to see a real Mormon wife, and that desire was presently gratified by the entrance of Mrs. North Number Ten, who was a rather good looking young woman, with an unnatural smile, and an underlying expression of perplexity and fretfulness. She was evidently desirous of conveying the impression that her position was a pleasant and happy one, but her efforts were marred by the behavior of Mary, who spoke to and regarded her all the time in a tender and pitying way which had the effect of confusing her greatly.

When she had gone, Mary sat for some moments deep in thought, and then said: "I wonder how these women can bear to look at their sisters 'who have not cast themselves away. How bitterly they must feel the humiliation of their position when they see Gentile wives secure in the love and affection of their husbands."

Henry thought of some wives of his acquaintance who were by no means secure in the love of their husbands, and expressed himself in a dubious assent.

"Don't you think," said Mary, fixing her great blue eyes upon him, "don't you think they must be very unhappy, Mr. Broome?"

"Really," replied Henry, "I have never given the subject much thought. You see there are so many women now-a-days who marry for money, or to get a home, or from a temporary fancy, and who don't seem to expect or care for any particular fidelity or love from their husbands, so long as they can have their own way."

Mary opened her eyes very wide at this.

"But Mr. Broome," she exclaimed, "a true woman can only love one man, and can only be happy when she knows that he loves her alone. I'm sure *I* should break my heart if I thought

John cared for any one else." And her eyes filled with tears at the very thought.

Henry muttered that he was afraid, if true women could only be happy under such circumstances, there must be a great number of false women in the world, for his experience was that dress and dissipation occupied more room in the modern female heart than anything else.

Of course Mary could not admit this for a moment, and proceeded to vindicate her sex from the charge of a tendency to frivolity and fickleness. In the course of her argument she grew quite warm, and was expatiating on the attributes of true womanhood, with sparkling eyes and glowing cheeks, when a light step was heard on the stairs, the door was flung open, and a handsome young fellow appeared on the threshhold, his face all aglow with love and happiness and blissful anticipation.

Mary sprang up, uttering a cry of delight, and was hurrying to meet the new comer with outstretched arms, when a sudden change that passed over him checked her midway.

You see he had rushed up the stairs, full of hope, and joy, and love, expecting to find his darling in the company of the friends who were to have traveled with her to the West. He had opened the door prepared to gather her to his heart—and he had found her enjoying an animated conversation with a very good looking—young—stranger. And seeing this, the demon Jealousy (always hovering about lovers) had made one clutch at his heart, and given it such a venomous gripe as drew the blood from his cheeks and the lovelight from his eyes, and hushed the fond words on his lips, and paralyzed his limbs, and left him standing there, no longer eager, flushed and rapturous, but pale, and cold, and suspicious, and angry.

This sudden—and to her inexplicable change—it was, that checked Mary as she was running, in a flutter of delight, to bury her pretty head in her lover's bosom. He recovered himself with an effort, and advancing, took her hand and kissed her cheek. But somehow everything was changed in the room. A shadow had fallen between them. The meeting, so long looked forward to, so eagerly anticipated, so often rehearsed in imagination, had come to pass, and it was a gloomy meeting after all. Mary had not at that moment any suspicion of the real cause of the change that had passed over the scene, but she knew that John was cold; that he was displeased; that he was not loving and kind. And then a sense of loneliness and desertion came on her, and as she looked into the darkened face of her jealous lover, her poor mouth quivered, and the corners drooped, and tears stole into her blue eyes.

It was all very unpleasant and disagreeable, and stupid and unkind, on John's part, of course. But it was not altogether unnatural, and so thought Henry Broome, who had risen when John entered, and now stood, resting his hand on the back of his chair, and looking, with a grave and somewhat rueful face, from one to the other. Of course *he* saw what the matter was, and he felt angry with John for his stupidity at first; but directly after he began to reflect a little, and then he found some excuse for him.

He would have retired at this juncture, but Mary, who was still puzzling over the lamentable change that was apparent in John's demeanor, now roused herself, and introduced the men to each other, adding that she was much indebted to Mr. Broome for his many kindnesses.

Mr. Rutter bowed coldly, and looked as though he could cheerfully attend the obsequies of Mr. Broome, who, on his part, looked and felt particularly uncomfortable, and not a little guilty. Muttering something about "pleasure of re-union,"—"must have much to talk over"—"prefer to be alone," etc., he was about to leave the room, when his inward monitor expostulated with him. What the inward monitor said was to this effect,—"Harry, you have got this little girl into this scrape, and its your business to get her out of it. You know you ought to have guarded against this sort of thing, and you didn't. Now do what you can to set this matter right, and don't let that jealous fellow have an excuse for making himself and his sweetheart miserable any longer."

Now, all this passed through his mind as he was backing toward the door, and the result was that just as he had placed his hand on the door-handle he turned, walked slowly back, and said quietly :

"Mr. Rutter, I can't help seeing that you were annoyed at finding me here, and I am afraid if I go away without saying what I have on my mind, that you and this young lady may be apt to have a misunderstanding. I should be very sorry indeed, to think that I had been the cause of any trouble between you, and I think it is my duty to assure you "—

Here he was interrupted by John Rutter, who had listened with impatience, and now turning to Mary asked, in an icy tone :

"Who *is* this gentleman, Miss Sheldon ? And how happens it that he assumes the position of a mediator between you and me ?"

This way of meeting his well-meant endeavors was not pleasant, and Henry began to feel rather angry, and inclined to make a sharp reply. But he restrained himself, and merely turned appealingly to Mary, who burst into tears, and exclaimed between her sobs :

"He was on the train from Echo—and when the train ran away—he threw things on the track—and told me not to be frightened—but I was—and I might have been *killed*, John—and made up my mind to die—and perhaps it would have been better for me—than to be treated so cruelly—" The rest was lost in a fresh fit of crying.

This explanation was not so luminous as to satisfy John Rutter, and Henry's good looks (which he could not help or disguise), only served to feed the flame of jealousy. John was naturally a good-tempered, pleasant, sympathetic, genial fellow ; but he was jealous, and just now things appeared to him to wear a very ugly look. He glanced moodily at Mary, not at all softened by her tears, and savagely at Henry, who was preparing to make a fresh attempt at pacification, when the door opened again with an uncompromising crash, and an apparition appeared in the doorway.

A young woman, of medium hight, graceful figure, pale face, lustrous dark eyes and heavy bands of black hair ; a young woman dressed in a riding habit of grey cloth, and carrying a whip in her muscular little hand; a young woman who took in the situation at a glance, and over whose beautiful features there passed a change as startling as that which had befallen Mary's lover, as she stepped into the apartment; a young woman, whose sudden and unceremonious entrance produced a singular effect upon John Rutter, who seemed suddenly to have transferred to himself all the confusion and awkwardness that had previously sat upon Henry. She advanced with a feline stride, her great flashing eyes fixed upon John with a look of scorn and triumph mingled, her red lips tightly compressed, her hand twitching nervously, and flapping her skirt with her whip. She looked at no one but John, but her eyes seemed to devour him, and he visibly shrunk, and became an abject and pitiable object under that burning gaze.

"So!" she at length exclaimed, when she had arrived close to the culprit, " So ! *This* is the cause of your visit to Ogden ! *This* is the contract you had to see about ! And *this* is the end of the game you have been playing with my heart !" She paused, half choking with emotion, indignation, regret, or grief, and put her hand to her throat. Her slight figure seemed to dilate with the passion that filled her, and as she erected herself over him, John Rutter seemed to shrink and collapse into the veriest insignificance.

While this was passing, Mary had sat silent with amazement, looking from one to the other, as doubting the evidence of her senses. Henry was no less amazed, but with his amazement was mingled admiration for the magnificent creature who had swept into the room like a thunderstorm, and stood there discharging electric bolts upon the head of Mary's lover. At last John managed to stammer out :

"Lucy, what brings you here. I thought you were in Elko ?"

Before she could reply, Mary rose, and passing between them, laid her hand upon John's shoulder, and confronted the enraged girl. She had ceased to cry, and there was a firmness in her face which Henry Broome had thought foreign to her character. She did not look at her lover, but she kept her hand on his shoulder, pressing it lightly, as she addressed the new comer:

"Yes," she said, "what do you want here? This is my betrothed husband. We have been engaged for years. He loves me; yes, he loves me better than you, for all your fiery eyes, and black hair, and pretty figure. I am to be his wife, not you. What do you want here?"

The girl whom John had addressed as Lucy, stepped back and flushed deeply, as Mary spoke. She was on the point of speaking, when Mary raised her hand to stay her, and resumed:

"Not yet! Wait a little, until I have done. I know my dear would not have forgotten me—no, not for a moment—unless he had been tempted. I know he never would have suffered another to take my place—no, not for a moment—unless that other had abused her opportunities. I know that *you* knew he was engaged, and that you set a snare for his feet, in the vanity and pride of your heart."

The little hand that rested on John's shoulder trembled, but she would not give way. Was she not battling for all that was dear to her? Was she not confronting the great crisis of her life? She continued:

"No; not yet. I have more to say. You thought you could win my dear away from me, with your great wild eyes. You thought you could break the heart of the silly little thing in the East who was engaged to him. But you never loved him truly—do not speak—I see it in your eyes; I read it in your looks; I know it by your bitter anger, which is wounded vanity, not love; and I tell you that you shall not have your way. You shall not break my heart or his!"

While she thus spoke, not loudly or with excitement, but earnestly and sweetly, Lucy remained gazing at her, glancing now and then at John, who sat with his head bowed down and buried in his hands.

When Mary ceased speaking, the other girl stood silent a moment, the color coming and going upon her cheeks, the light rising and fading in her eyes. It was plain to be seen that a great struggle was going on in her mind. It was plain to be seen that her good and evil genii were contending for the mastery. It was plain to be seen in the dark clouds that passed over her face, and in the softened expression that alternated with them. She looked at Mary, and the hardness of her gaze melted. She glanced at John's bowed head, and her lips closed cruelly. Three times she opened her mouth to speak, and as often the words died away unuttered. At length she said, in a constrained, unnatural voice :

" Ask him ! Let him speak for himself."

At this appeal, John Rutter shuddered, and plucking his hands from his face, rose and faced her, catching and retaining Mary's hand as he did so. He was very pale and haggard. He seemed to have grown ten years older in the last few minutes. There were deep lines about his mouth and eyes, and his features looked drawn and pinched, like those of one who has just passed through a long and severe illness. When he essayed to speak his lips were so dry that he was compelled to moisten them before he could proceed. When he began to speak he looked neither at Mary nor Lucy, but kept his eyes bent upon the ground at his feet. And this is what he said :

" I have nothing to urge in my defense· Mary, I have wronged you cruelly; but, Mary, you have wronged *her*. You were absent, and I was foolish. I don't think—that is, I did not tell her—that I was engaged to you. But I never thought she (it was noticeable that he never spoke of Lucy directly) cared for me much. I never thought seriously about it, indeed. We were thrown together, and—and—I was—no, I won't say I was fascinated, for I went into the business with my eyes open. I didn't think it would ever come to this. I didn't think it would come to anything—till I found that I had gone further than I ought to have gone, and that *you* were on your way here."

There was a painful silence, and then Mary, now pale as her rival, and with, oh, such a look of wretchedness and pain on her sweet face, gently disengaged her hand from his and resumed :

" Don't stop there, John. Tell me all. Tell me the worst at once."

John gave a great gasp, and for the first time time looked full at Lucy. He hesitated, but was about to resume his confession, with such an expression as a man on the rack might wear, when Lucy, who had been studying his face attentively, cried :

" Hold ! You have sinned, and are punished. I have trusted, and am punished. Perhaps I also sinned. But I am alone, and can live alone. When I am gone you two will outlive this bitterness. I will not interfere between you."

She stopped, struggled again with herself, and resumed, in a low, sad tone :

" He never loved me. It was but a foolish flirtation, and none but a wild creature such as I am would have made this trouble. His heart has always been yours, and always will be. Forget that this has happened, and let all be as though I had not intruded here."

She turned, and moved to the door. Reaching it, she looked back over her shoulder at the two lovers, who stood a little apart, pale, silent, and perplexed; and in that look Henry Broome read the extent of her sacrifice, and his spirit went forth toward the woman who had offered up her own life-happiness upon the altar of her noble love.

CHAPTER IV.

THE CUP AND THE LIP.

Everybody who travels at all knows the thriving little town of Shoo Fly, in Nevada. Perhaps they may not recognize it under that name, but the place itself would be the same no matter what you called it; and when it has been described none will hesitate for a moment as to *which* town is meant. There are a great many new towns on the line of the railroad; mushroom cities that seem to have sprung up from the crumbs dropped by the boarding cars of the construction trains, and which took their chances on the wisdom of location and the advantages of surroundings. Some of these flourished for a few weeks or months, became conceited and saucy, erected a huge

caravanserai and a huge feed store, and then rapidly declined
and became pitiable and melancholy deserts of lumber and canvas.

But Shoo Fly was not one of these ephemeral growths. It
was so long established that the shingles on the roofs had be-
gun to turn grey and slate-colored, and the citizens could boast
(as they did with pardonable pride) that they possessed a baby
whose mother had been married in the town. This fact always
acted as a crusher upon the pretensions of the people of other
and neighboring burghs, for you see it was one of those stub-
born things which no amount of emulation would enable them
to rival, much less surpass ; and knowing this, the people of
Shoo Fly perhaps presumed somewhat on their good fortune.

Shoo Fly was well situated, near a fine river, and not far
from an abundance of timber. There were mineral dis-
tricts of much promise within easy access, and a lively trade
was established already, with a rapidly settling farming country on the one side, a rapidly developing mining country on
another side, and a rapidly building railroad country on a third
side. On the whole, Shoo Fly might fairly be styled a thriving
place, and possessing, moreover, the gravity and weight which
age gives (it was within a week of being a twelvemonth old)
was naturally looked up to by its neighbors.

Its exterior and material aspect was plain, not ornamental.
One street, two dozen stores, two wooden hotels, two livery
stables, six saloons, and a round house and machine shop belonging to the railway, about completed the picture. But Shoo
Fly had two aspects : its railroad aspect and its stage aspect.
The first was commonplace and tame. Everybody knows it.
A wooden platform, a hurry and bustle, a clanging and whis-
tling, and wheezing, a smell of oil, and a pervading sensation of
cinders, a rapid freight clerk, a stern ticket clerk, a clicking telegraph clerk, a bawling roadmaster.

The stage aspect was different. You passed down a little
street, about six yards long, and came upon the stage office at
the back of the town. You turned a corner, and there was a
dining saloon, always filled at train time with a hungry crowd,
either just about to leave by the train, having come in by the

stage, or just about to leave by the stage, having come in by
the train. There was a peculiarity about the stage passengers
never noticeable in the train passengers. Trains have a level-
ing tendency. They repress individuality and stifle the exhibi-
tion of idiosyncracies. Everybody feels just the same when
traveling by a train. The same general griminess, the same lia-
bility to attract cinders in the eyes, the same tendency to ex-
aggerate the angularity of the seats, the same sleepiness and
the same inability to sleep, affect everybody.

But on the stages at Shoo Fly it was not so. Those stages—
great clumsy, red vehicles, with dusty leather curtains in place
of windows, and the most horribly uncomfortable internal ar-
rangements—went far out into the wild parts of the country.
Some of them climbed high into the mountains, amid snow and
ice; some of them traversed the dreary alkali plains, where
smothering heat and dust made journeying a torture, and
where the sand and sage brush extend for melancholy miles
on miles, barren, desolate and depressing. And the passengers
were queer looking customers. Here would be one wrapped in
a huge blanket coat, and wearing great boots reaching to the
thighs. There would be another, buttoned up close in ample
linen duster, with auxiliary pocket handkerchief tied loosely
about the neck, and hat slouched over so as to "shed" the
sand and dust. There were miners, and farmers, and graziers,
and lawyers, and gamblers, and laborers, and mill men, and dro-
vers, and engineers, and a very few women, who always ruled
the stage passengers with an absolute sway, and did with everybody (except the driver) pretty much as they pleased. Some
of the passengers have Henry or Spencer rifles with them, and
look as though they knew how to use them.

At times the stages in certain quarters run (or have run)
risks from Indians. In other quarters they run (or have run)
risks from road agents. In the former case they generally give
a good account of the aggressors. In the latter case the aggressors generally give a good account of them. The reason of
this is that Indians seek scalps; road agents merely treasure
boxes. The drivers do not consider themselves bound to fight
for the company's property, but they need no persuasion to in-

duce them to fight for their own lives. The passengers regard the matter in much the same light, and the result is that the road agents thrive while the Indians do not. So much for philosophy and prudence.

The stages left Shoo Fly sometimes twice and sometimes three times a day. But whether they left twice or twenty times there would always have been found a sufficient number of citizens to constitute the knot of spectators that watched each vehicle's departure, and stood looking silently after it until it disappeared, with a solemn and reflective gaze.

Such were the principal outward features of interest in Shoo Fly. Of its inner life—its social position—much might be said. Shoo Fly was respectable and progressive. It had its weaknesses—its faro bank or two—and its other headquarters of dissipation. But it permitted no rowdyism, and the men who had tried to bully Shoo Fly, or commit any disorderly acts within its limits, would have taken a greater risk than most men care to encounter. The Shoo Fly people were practical and full of business. They were warm-hearted, hospitable and generous. They were rough and straightforward in their ways, fond of poker, not averse to whisky toddies, addicted to cigars; but, take them altogether, perhaps as jovial, honest, whole-souled a little community as an energetic man need wish to settle among.

At this particular period Shoo Fly was considerably excited over a brand-new sensation, and the male population was discussing the affair with much gusto, though with a kind of natural gravity, too. Stealing cattle was not of itself a novelty. There was a fair grazing country in the valley that lay to the right of the town, and cattle had vanished thence before. But never before had a woman been caught stealing cattle, and this it was that so excited Shoo Fly.

The long and short of it was that Lucy Draper had been arrested in the act of driving off a band of cattle, and that she was to be tried for the offense. Now, Lucy Draper was in some sort a popular institution, and was regarded by Shoo Fly and the whole country round about with a feeling very near akin to universal admiration. Lucy was young and handsome. She owned a ranch in a fertile valley. She lived alone, or at least without other company than an old female servant. She was a daring horsewoman, a dead shot with gun, revolver and rifle, an intrepid huntress, a fluent talker, and a scorner of all conventional usages. She had lived in the valley for several years, and everybody knew her for miles around, though nobody understood her. The women abused her mercilessly, but the men liked her, and did not mind saying so. She had been in many scrapes, and, to say the truth, had more than once made the acquaintance of the District Attorney. But with all her wildness nobody had a word to say against her reputation as a *woman*, and she was looked upon generally as a social puzzle. This, however, was the wildest and worst undertaking she had yet ventured upon, and consequently the excitement was considerable. It was, indeed, remarked that since her return from that trip on the railroad East, she had been much more eccentric and reckless than before, and some of the older inhabitants had ventured to expostulate with her, though unavailingly. Had she been a man there can be no question that it would have gone hard with her, for cattle stealing was a capital offense in the eyes of the people of this region. But, being what she was, her crime was regarded rather as a comical escapade than as a serious matter, and the occasion of the trial became quite an excuse for a holiday.

The knots that assembled around the Court House, and the express office, and the railroad depot, were all discussing this subject. At one place the express agent was narrating the history of her famous ball, to which she had invited all the settlers for twenty miles around, ran in debt for the entertainment, and when her favorite mare was attached by the Sheriff, stole it out of the stable at night, leaped a six-foot fence, and distanced her pursuers gallantly. At another place an eager group were listening to the story of her shooting exploits—the most notable of which was the discomfiture of a rowdy who had mistaken her character, and meeting her alone on horseback one day had offered to insult her. She had put a ball through his right arm, knocked him off his horse with the butt of her pistol, and seized his steed as spoils of war. Another time, when a party of gay

young fellows conspired to make her "tight," thinking she
could not stand liquor, she drank them all into helplessness,
tied them in their chairs, blackened their faces, and so left
them—to be the butts of the whole district forever after.

These stories might have been continued indefinitely, but for
the fact that the time for the Court to open had arrived, and as
this event was what everybody had been waiting for, the good
people of Shoo Fly trooped off to the Court House to enjoy the
proceedings.

There was an additional source of interest in the fact that
a new lawyer was to undertake Lucy's defense. He was a
young man, had not been long in the neighborhood, but had
made many friends by his genial ways and his knowledge of
poker. His name was Broome, and rumor said that he was
sweet upon his fair client, who certainly treated him with more
consideration and regard than she showed to any of the young
men of the district.

When the prisoner entered the Court there was a loud buzz
of curiosity and admiration. She was dressed in black, and
looked very quiet and demure. Her heavily-fringed eyelids
were cast modestly down, her black hair was arranged neatly
under a sober little hat, and she certainly looked as little like a
desperate character as could well be imagined.

The jury were empaneled, Mr. Broome making very few
challenges, and the Prosecuting Attorney arose to state the case.
It was very plain, and he felt assured of a conviction. The
prisoner had been caught in the act of driving a band of cattle
belonging to Abijah Jones, and had attempted to resist the
officers. He would be able to show that the defendant was a
person of bad character (a murmur of dissent in the Court) and
he should press for a summary conviction.

Then the witnesses were called. Abijah Jones, the owner of
the stolen cattle, unfortunately for himself bore the character of
a disagreeable old curmudgeon. He was prosperous but penu-
rious. Old and ugly; mean looking and spiteful looking. He
did not impress the jury at all favorably, but his evidence was
incontrovertible, and cross-examination failed to shake him.

Then the Deputy Sheriff, who had arrested Lucy, was exam-

ined, and testified to having found her riding in the rear of the
cattle, and to her defiance of the law, which was carried even
so far as the drawing of a pistol on him. This looked grave,
and the jury were compelled to take a glance at the defendant.
Her demure and innocent aspect evidently refreshed them much,
and they smiled pityingly on the Deputy Sheriff. Mr. Broome
declined to ask the witness any questions, and one or two others
having been examined, the Prosecuting Attorney said that was
his case.

Then there was a buzz, hushed suddenly as the young lawyer
rose and prepared to address the jury for the defense.

He commenced by drawing a vivid picture of a western
homestead. He represented a happy and united family, pros-
pering by their own exertions, and respected by their neighbors.
Then he showed how unexpected troubles came upon this family.
How sickness struck down the children one after the other;
how droughts, and floods, and vermin ruined the crops, and
wasted the land; how at length the head of the family was compelled to throw up his old homestead; and how they set forth
on a long journey to the far West. He described the perils and
privations of that journey across the Plains. He appealed to
the experience of the jury, many, perhaps most, of whom, had
passed through the same dangers. He told how the travellers
had camped, one fatal night, near a certain ford, and how the
cruel Indians had swept down upon them at daylight, and had
murdered the emigrants—all save two, one of whom was the
prisoner, and the other a sorely wounded man, who possessed
just strength enough to carry his little charge out of danger,
and then sank and died. He narrated how this orphan child
had been found by strangers, who brought her on with them.
He painted the loneliness of her childhood; the lack of a mother's
advice and a father's vigilance. He showed how the native
independence of the girl had rebelled against her condition;
how her high spirit had chafed against the tyranny of strangers,
who made a reproach of her misfortunes, and treated her as a
bond-servant. He dwelt eloquently upon the difficulties that
had surrounded her; called the attention of the jury to the
beauty with which nature had endowed her; spoke of the temp-

tations which beset a girl without relatives to help her; commented on the brave spirit she had shown in determining to earn her own living on her own land; and concluded by an appeal to the chivalry and humanity of the jury, which called forth a storm of applause.

When he sat down Henry Broome had said simply nothing in relation to the cattle stealing; but he had gained his point. The Prosecuting Attorney (whose heart was not in the case) glanced at the jury, smiled, and declined to reply.

The judge summed up briefly, stating that the case was very clear, and that the jury could not hesitate as to their decision.

The jury retired, whispered together for a few minutes, and then declared that they were agreed.

The verdict, cheerfully delivered by the foreman, as an opinion which did credit alike to the hearts and the heads of himself and his fellows, was—"*Not Guilty!*"

It is true that this decision was in direct opposition to the evidence, and in defiance of the law governing the case. But it was received with rapture by the people who filled the Court, and cheer after cheer resounded as they filed into the open air, and shook hands with the successful counsel, and Lucy, and each other, with as much inward satisfaction and actual joy as though they had all been running for Congress, and had all been elected by immense majorities.

Harry Broome was the hero of the hour, and received the earnest congratulations of all Shoo Fly. Even Bill Burke, the blacksmith, who was the strongest man in the place, and was so terribly hen-pecked by his mite of a wife that he never dared to call his soul his own, was so exhilarated that he actually asked Harry to come and dine with him—and immediately after stood appalled at the magnitude of his daring. But the sweetest triumph for Harry was when Lucy approached him, and laying her hand upon his arm thanked him, with tears in her eyes. Lucy was not one of your crying women, and even on this occasion it seemed to Harry that in the look she gave him there was more of a tender pity for himself than gladness for her own escape. Yet it made him very happy, for to tell the truth, he had received little encouragement heretofore from her.

When she left Ogden, after that stormy scene, he had followed her, scarcely knowing or caring why. It was a case of love at first sight; a kind of love much more common than is generally believed, and much more lasting than many other kinds of love. After what had passed, she could not treat him as a stranger, for he had become acquainted with her secret. But though she soon grew to like him, and to take pleasure in his company, and though she used her influence to persuade him into abandoning his wild, useless life, she would hold out no hope to him. With instinctive delicacy he refrained from alluding to the past, trusting that Time would heal her heartwounds, and being content to keep himself before her as much as possible. He had been bred to the law in the East, but had early acquired a distaste for the profession, and a quarrel with his family had set him adrift, to wander aimlessly on the frontiers, and, to pick up much more evil than good. This girl, wild though she was, disliked wildness in others. She saw that there was a foundation of energy and sound sense in young Broome, and she urged him to make a better use of his time. He would have done anything she told him to do, so settled quietly down in Shoo Fly and burnished up his early reminiscences of law practice, with what result, so far as Lucy was concerned, has already appeared.

Harry helped the late prisoner on her horse, and she rode off to her ranch. He looked after her as long as she was visible, and then walked over to his little office, and lighting a cigar sat down to ponder. He had made an important step, he thought. The ground was well broken, and the future was less difficult. He had no fears for Lucy, for wild as she was, he felt confident that marriage would settle her, and that she would make a good wife. As for himself, he had given up all his old dissipated habits, and had already obtained the reputation of a steady, rising young fellow. His own path seemed clear enough.

Perhaps he would not have felt quite so confident had he observed the two travelers who had just then passed his office,

4

and turned into a restaurant hard by. They were travel-stained, dirty, fatigued looking fellows, and sat down wearily and called for food. They were by no means prepossessing in appearance, and though plenty of rough characters passed through Shoo Fly every day, these would have attracted something more than a casual glance from the bright, resolute eyes of the active citizen who officiated as Sheriff of the county, had he happened to see them. One of these men was tall, burly, dark, heavy-bearded. The other was small, wiry, yellow-faced, and wore a straw-colored goatee. In short, the two men were our old-acquaintances, Messrs. Belto and Cobbins, who had miraculously escaped death in the catastrophe of the railroad bridge (the fortune that usually attends the Devil's Own having attended them thus far)—and finding Utah too warm for them, had determined to try their luck in Nevada.

The restaurant was full of customers, and as the principal subject of conversation was the trial which had taken place that morning, the new arrivals soon became acquainted with the facts. Neither of them took much notice of the comments which were freely made upon the power and ability displayed by the young lawyer. They were naturally prejudiced against lawyers, and regarded them as nuisances. But Mr. Belto was much taken with the story of Lucy Draper, and asked many questions about her career and exploits, which latter seemed to amuse him greatly. Taking a stroll through the town after dinner, he confided to his partner that he was "kinder stuck arter that there gal." From the description he had received he was inclined to believe that she was a young woman after his own heart, and the more he thought of the matter the more impressed did he become with a desire to make her acquaintance. Mr. Cobbins, never addicted to sentiment of any kind, paid little attention to the other's remarks, being mentally engaged in discussing the "show" for starting a little game. He had already satisfied himself that the customs of Kill-me-Quick were not the customs of Shoo Fly, and that caution and circumspection would be necessary in the latter place. But he still hoped that something might be made out of the visit, and was casting about in his mind for a promising project. To him, thus occupied, his partner spoke.

" Cobbins," said he thoughtfully, " a gal o' that sort'd likely have a few twenties around her place. Likewise a good horse or two. Also purvisions. They say she lives all alone by herself, and that there's nobody round but an old woman, or somethin' o' that kind. I've more than half a mind to pay her a visit to-night. Wot do you think?"

" Make the d—d place too hot to hold us," replied Mr. Cobbins sententiously.

" Who's to know us, you flat? We've on'y been here a couple of hours or so, and not more'n half a dozen has set eyes on us. Strikes me its a bully lay-out, and I'm —— if 1 don't do it, too !"

Thus, with a smart slap upon his thigh, did Mr. Belto proclaim that his mind was made up on the subject, and as Mr. Cobbins always deferred to him, as the more daring and original in his conceptions, and, as also the more capable, physically, he yielded on this occasion, after a brief remonstrance, to which he was moved more by a reluctance to abandon a certain gambling scheme he had just mapped out, than from any apprehensions as to the result of the visit. So it was arranged that they should call on Lucy that evening, at a somewhat later hour than ladies usually receive company.

Now it so happened that Henry Broome had determined upon visiting Lucy this evening also, and as her place was only about six miles from Shoo Fly, he rode out quietly after dinner, and spent a couple of hours with her. She was much kinder to-night than she had ever been before, and as they sat and talked in her homely little parlor, while the old servant mended stockings in a corner of the room, (Lucy insisting on her presence, with a prudent regard for her reputation), Henry was quite happy, and more hopeful than ever.

Lucy's conversation was not at all like Mary Sheldon's. She possessed a vigorous intellect, and though it had been little cultivated her thoughts were original and daring, and her expression confident and easy. Henry could talk to her freely about his affairs; could expostulate with her on her recklessness; could speak plainly with her about her peculiar ideas of the rights of property; and was never afraid of offending her by

his plainness, or of getting beyond her capacity on any subject. She admired him for his candor, good sense, and strength
of mind. She liked him for his freedom from that snickering
spooniness which afflicted most of the young men when in her
presence. But she had not yet recovered from the shock of her
parting with John Rutter, though she had resolutely determined to crush the memory of him from out her heart.

So the young couple sat and chatted pleasantly, yet soberly,
and when Harry at length rose to take his leave he was perfectly satisfied with the result of his visit. He mounted his
horse, lighted a cigar, and rode slowly homeward, full of bright
anticipations, and building castles in the air at an astonishing
rate. He might have been in the saddle a quarter of an hour
or so—he never could tell exactly how long it was, he had been
so lost in thought—when the report of a pistol rang upon the
night air and startled him from his reverie. The sound came
from the direction of the house he had left. There was no
other dwelling within three or four miles, and he could not,
therefore, be mistaken. Half-defined fears crowded into his
mind as he turned his horse's head and galloped back.

When he left Lucy she stood on the porch, watching his re-
ceding form, for a few moments, and then re-entered the house,
and seated herself, with a half-suppressed sigh of weariness and
vexation. She found the crushing out process harder than she
had contemplated. The attentions and the presence of Harry,
so far from erasing the memory of the past, only recalled it
more vividly, and often as she sat with him fancy would replace his well known features with the still better remembered
lineaments of her lost love. She fought against it bravely, and
it was because she fought so bravely that she was vexed and
distressed to find how slow her progress was. This evening she
felt strangely downcast. She had not noticed it when Harry
was present, but now that she was alone again her isolation impressed itself on her more than ever before. Her mind re-
verted to the scene of the morning, and she went over the trial
and Harry's speech, and the verdict, and the congratulations of
the people, again. Somehow she experienced no sort of satisfaction from her acquittal. She began to despise herself, and to

feel ashamed of her wild pranks as she had not done before.
The truth was that Harry's influence was making itself felt, and
the first step to reformation—dissatisfaction with the existing
state of things—was being made.

She was suddenly roused from her brooding by a scream of
mortal fear from the old woman, who sat near the door, and
looking up she saw the servant's eyes fixed, with a terrified expression, upon a man's face which was peering in through the
half-opened portal. It was an ugly and a villainous face, but it
did not frighten Lucy. She sprang at once for her pistol,
which lay, ready loaded, on the mantel-piece; but at the same
moment the door of the back room opened suddenly, and another man appeared, while the first dashed forward toward
her. She had secured her pistol, but this complication of the
attack confused her, and her first shot was fired almost at random. Before she could cock the weapon again her arms were
gripped tightly from behind, it was wrested from her, and she
was forced, panting, into a chair, and securely bound with
cords. The old servant continuing to scream, Mr. Cobbins
knocked her down with the butt of the pistol, and gagged her.
The two ruffians then turned their attention to Lucy, who now
sat still and composed, looking them both in the face boldly
and sternly. Mr. Belto eyed her with undisguised admiration.

"Mons'us putty gal!" he observed to Mr. Cobbins, who was
already instituting a search into the resources of the establishment; "mighty handy with the pistol, too." Then, addressing
Lucy, conversationally: "And so you're the gal as corrals
stock, are you? Well! now! ef that don't beat my time!"
and he gazed at his captive thoughtfully, and helped himself to
a chew of tobacco.

Lucy said nothing, but her eyes flashed in a way that would
have boded no good to Mr. Belto had her arms been free. Mr.
Cobbins was a man of business, and here interfered.

"Stow that d—d truck, Belto, and help me go through the
house. Say, you," addressing Lucy brutally, "where in the
—— do you keep your dust?"

"You git out," responded Mr. Belto, coolly pushing his companion aside. "That ain't no kind o' way to talk. My dear,

we are hard up, and wants to make a raise. I know you wouldn't refuse to help us, but you'r too tired to get about, and we're in a hurry. Where is the key of the money drawer, eh?"

Lucy held her tongue. Mr. Cobbins blasphemed. Mr. Belto began to "rile" and the servant began to recover her senses.

Just at this moment the door opened again, and Harry Broome entered the room.

The two gamblers raised their weapons at sight of him, and were about to fire when they recognized him, simultaneously. Belto uttered a furious cry and his companion a terrific oath, and both sprang upon him, by one consent. He had not time to draw his pistol, and could only grapple with them. There was a wild struggle, a stifled cursing and panting, a stamping and blundering here and there, a knocking down of tables and chairs, and then Harry lay on the floor, with Mr. Belto's powerful knee upon his breast, and Mr. Belto's powerful hands holding his arms as if in a vice. Mr. Belto's face at this moment was not a pleasant sight to see. It was the face of a triumphant fiend, all malignity and revenge, and cruelty, and sense of power. He called for cords and bound Harry firmly. Then he rose, looked at him murderously, drew a deep breath and cocked his revolver.

"So, you durn skunk!" he said then, "you thought you'd got away with Slaughterhouse Jack, did you? You burned Kill-me-Quick, did you? You uncoupled the train, and thought you'd sent us to hell, did you? Now I'll send *you* there!"

It was evident that he meant murder. Lucy could see that in his eye, and so could Harry. It was evident that he only delayed the shot for the pleasure of tantalizing his victim. But Mr. Cobbins had a word to say also, and that word was—"Aint you a —— fool, Belto? What good will it do to blow that skunk's head off now? Bring him away with us, and *I'll* show you how to put him through."

Mr. Belto looked at his partner for a moment as if he suspected him of an intention to rob him of his prey; but there was that in Mr. Cobbins' eyes which reassured him, and he replied—"Dunno but what you're right, Cob. Guess we'll put him on one of the horses and take him along."

Lucy had witnessed the unmistakable hatred evinced by the gamblers toward Harry, with amazement and perplexity. It was evident that they knew him, and that they had some old grudge against him; and it was also evident that they were bent on a bloody vengeance now they had him in their hands. She felt that all hope of intercession on her part was vain, and yet she felt impelled to make an effort. "Let him go, you brutes," she cried passionately, "you are welcome to all you can find here. But if you harm *him* I'll have the country on your track before daylight."

Mr. Cobbins looked ferociously at the girl, and drew his knife. He evidently thought her threats were not to be despised, and that the best way to avert danger was to silence her effectually. But Belto would not hear of this. He liked her pluck, and he cared for nothing now he had Harry in his power. He motioned to Cobbins to put up his knife, and proceeded to haul the prisoner to his feet, preparatory to placing him on horseback.

Harry saw Lucy's danger and told her not to mind him. If the fellows killed him it wouldn't matter much, and it was no use making a fuss over what couldn't be helped. He had faced death too often to fear it, and she mustn't fret.

She spoke no more. She only exchanged one glance with him as he was being borne to the door, and in that glance he read her assurance that come what might, he would be avenged.

The gamblers gagged him, set him on his own horse, and having secured some provisions from the house, and taken whatever of value they could find, prepared to start. When they were in the saddle, Mr. Cobbins delivered his farewell thus—

"You can tell this young man's friends, ef he's got any, that we've saved them the expenses of a funeral. They won't see *him* again, unless they go where he'll mighty soon be."

With that ominous parting the scene closed. The tramp of the horses rang out on the still night, growing fainter and fainter, and Lucy sat, bound fast to her chair, gazing into the thick darkness through the open doorway.

CHAPTER V.

THE FORTY-MILE DESERT.

The sun was setting. Seen through the heated atmosphere that quivered over the arid plain he resembled a large red-hot cannon ball, and fancy might have suggested the possibility of his setting fire to the range of hills whose uppermost ridge his lower limb was touching. The scene over which his last hot gleams shot was a dreary and depressing scene. Far as the eye could reach extended a bleak desert. Low hillocks swelled at intervals along the horizon, and broke the flatness of the expanse. But no tree, nor shrub, nor green thing, nor human being, nor dwelling house of man, nor running stream, existed there. It was the Great Desert of Nevada, sometimes known as the Forty-mile Desert. Alkali, lava and sand; patches of sage brush, sickly and weak of growth, scattered here and there; broad stretches of bare, hard earth—and that was all. The midday sun had been pouring his rays down with intolerable fierceness upon the naked ground. At evening the ground gave back to the atmosphere some portion of its superabundant heat, and the plain was stifling all the night. Such breezes as ventured to cross the desert were speedily robbed of their coolness and their invigorating qualities, and wandered languidly and feebly at last, flushing the parched cheek of the traveler, and scorching like blasts from the throat of a furnace. No living thing made the desert its home. Even the shrill note of the cricket was not heard there, and the active cotton-tail rabbit fled the accursed place.

A horrible silence hovered over the desolate region, a lurid gloom was settling down upon it, as three horsemen left the confines of the fertile lands and struck out into the plain. The fine alkali dust rose in suffocating clouds as their horses' feet fell noiselessly, and the air was so filled with this dust that it penetrated the clothing, the eyes, noses, ears and mouths of the travelers, and caused them to gasp for breath.

Of the three men the two who rode on the outside were conversing at intervals. The one in the middle sat sullenly, with his head on his breast, and was silent. A closer inspection would have shown that the silent rider was a captive, for his ankles were lashed together under his horse's belly, his hands were bound in front of him, and his horse was being led by a line fastened to the saddle-bow of the taller of his companions.

They rode on and on, into the desert and the night. The alkali dust hung in gray clouds upon their track, and settled very slowly after they had passed. Their horses coughed and tossed their heads, plainly evincing their uneasiness at the situation. The sun disappeared behind the low hills in the distance, and a burning wind crept over the plain, parching the lips of the riders and closing the pores of the skin as with the breath of fever.

At length the captive raised his head and spoke.

"What are you going to do with me, you two?"

Mr. Belto referred to his partner.

"What are we going to do with him, Cobbins?"

Mr. Cobbins cleared his mouth of the alkali dust as well as he could, and replied by asking a question in his turn.

"Did you ever hear of Jack Slade?"

"I have heard of an infernal scoundrel of that name," replied the captive.

Mr. Cobbins waved away the epithet, as irrelevant, and asked again:

"And did you ever hear of what he did to Jules Berg?"

"No!" was the reply.

"Well, then, I'll tell you; it'll help to pass away the time, and it'll may be serve as an answer to your question. Mr. Jack Slade was a Division Superintendent on the old Overland Stage Line. A mos' peart an' lively man *he* was, and stood no back talk from any one. He was all-fired quick with the pistol, and had taken a baker's dozen of scalps afore he met Jules Berg. Now, Berg was one o' them there skunks as thinks they has a right to interfere everywhere—as *you* interfered with us, you ——, (blank filled to suit the fancy), and Jack, he wasn't agoin' to put up with such goin's on. They had a kind of ruction once, and Jack had to take water; but he never forgot

nothin' and he just had it in for that Berg. Well, his time came
around. Some on his pals, they got Berg off to a quiet station,
by a plant, and they sent word to Slade as how he was corraled.
May be the old man didn't put on an extra stage to get there.
Oh, no! Nor he didn't drive all night, so's to lose no time!
Anyhow, he arrove at the station, and there he found that
skunk Berg fixed up as slick as could be. You see the boys,
knowin' Jack was kinder pressed for time, had got things all
ready aforehand, and, when he come, there was Jules tied up to
a post in the corral, as handy as could be. Jack eases his mind
a bit, cussin' him, and then he sets to and shoots him, little by
little. Jack was an awful good shot, and could put the balls
just where he wanted, and he'd fire a bullet through Jules' leg, or
arm, or shoulder, or wot not, and cuss 'im a spell, and go in and
take a drink with the boys—there was quite a crowd to see the
sport—and then go out and take another shot; and so on.
There's no denyin' that that there Jules was game, for he wouldn't
squeal, though he was fairly riddled. Jack had put two and
twenty balls into him without killin' him, and might ha' kept
the game up longer, on'y he'd taken just 's many drinks as he
fired shots, and was getting mad at Jules' not sayin' nothin',
nor screechin'. So at last he goes up to him, and after kickin'
him about a bit, and cussin' him all he wanted, he puts the pistol in his mouth and finishes the business. He kept Jules' ears
as a sort of remembrancer, an' ef ever you wanted to put Jack
in a good humor afterwards, all you had to do was to ask him
to tell you how he got them ears."

Harry Broome showed no discomposure as Mr. Cobbins concluded this revolting story (unhappily true, every word of it),
but remarked: "And that's the kind of 'game' you're going to
play with me, is it? "Well, there's one consolation: I was on
the Vigilance Committee that hanged your friend Jack Slade."

Mr. Cobbins drew a deep breath, and regarded his captive
with additional fervency.

"Oh," he said, pleasantly, "you were, were you? Well,
now, I'm glad to know *that*. It don't make it any worse for
you, cause you see we mean to make it about as rough as
rough can be, anyhow. But its a comfort to know that we'll

be fulfillin' a dooty as well as enjoyin' a soothin' pleasure when we help you to hand in your checks. Stranger, you're a dangerous carakter, and Society can*not* put up with you no longer!" With this protest on behalf of Society, Mr. Cobbins relapsed into silence, and the three men rode on, and on, into the desert and the night.

About midnight they halted to take a few hours' rest before entering upon the business of the morning. The captive was informed that he would not require any breakfast, and that it was not worth while to waste a supper on him, as he would hardly have time to digest it. The gamblers, however, were well supplied with whisky, and had also some crackers with them, on which they supped with much apparent satisfaction. The horses were next carefully hobbled, and the prisoner being laid on his back, his captors took their stations on either side of him, and in a few minutes fell asleep.

Harry, in spite of the awful nature of his position, felt drowsy. He was fatigued with the long ride, and his ankles and wrists were chafed and sore. He did not wish to go to sleep, but the heat and the fatigue, and the heavy breathing of the wretches by his side, combined to lull him into a feverish, dreamy state. For perhaps an hour he lay thus, becoming wide awake at intervals, then dropping into an uneasy slumber; but gradually the drowsy feeling wore off, the nervous forces asserted their supremacy, and he was fully roused.

Then he began to think. He went back over his whole past life in detail. Through childhood, school life, college life, law office life, wild frontier life, up to the meeting with Mary Sheldon. There he lingered a little, wondering how she got on with John, and whether he was at all jealous now. From her his mind passed naturally to Lucy, and he recalled his first meeting with her, and her passionate agony, and his sudden admiration of her. From that his memory passed to Shoo Fly, and the trial, and the verdict, and he wondered how those jurymen would feel if they knew the young lawyer they admired so much was lying out on the desert awaiting a cruel and violent death. The thought of death caused him to revert to the story of Jules Berg, and he began to consider whether Berg's stoi-

cism was real or whether the shooting was not so painful
after all.   He remembered having read that men on the battle-
field who were killed by gunshot wounds always looked peaceful and quiet after death, while those who had been stabbed
showed the traces of great suffering in their faces. How long
would it take to kill him? And was there not a chance that
they might do it by accident on the third or fourth shot? What
would become of his body?   Would it lie there in the desert till
the flesh was all gone, and the bones were bleached and white?
And would there be any search made for him?   Would Lucy—
just then his memory sprang with a bound to the last time he
had seen her, and he recalled the eloquent look she had given
him as she sat bound in her chair, and they were taking him
out of the door. Of course she would raise the country. But
it would be too late. They would never track his murderers,
and if they found what was left of him it would only be to
cause additional misery. No! on the whole it was better that
he should be left where he fell. A hot gust passed over his face
and changed the current of his thoughts. Where was he going?
Was there another world? And would he remember his old
life there? Was he going to punishment or rest? A world of
shadows or a world of existence? Would he bound at once
into the new existence, with all his intelligence alive, or would
he wake as a new-born child wakes here? Would death come
as an annihilator or as an illuminator? As the Shadow fell
upon him would he begin to see through the curtain that veils
the future from mortal eyes, and commence life there before he
had quitted life here? Would he be able, in the spirit form, to
watch over Lucy—as he was thinking thus, a sound caught his
ear.

It was so still there in the desert that the faintest noise was
instantly audible. He had heard the soft tread of the horses,
muffled by the yielding soil, but the sound which now broke the
silence was different from that. He listened intently, all his
nerves stretched to their utmost tension, his breath coming
short and quick. It was but a faint sound. A light, regular
beat, falling on his ear; and yet he knew from the first that it
was an important sound for him. Softly, cautiously, it ap-

proached. He could not raise his head, nor see on either side of him, but he felt that it—whatever it was—was guided by some strong intelligence, and that it was friendly to him. Softly, stealthily it approached. The suspense was becoming intolerable, and he closed his eyes. But he could not keep them closed, and when he looked up again he felt, as men do often feel, that some one was near him, though he could see nothing. The creeping sound had ceased for a moment. Then a shadow. fell on his face, and a warm hand glided over his mouth.

The shadow fell darker, he glanced upward—and Lucy's eyes were looking down into his, in the dim starlight.

It was unnecessary to caution him, for his faculties were at once under full control. She motioned him to lie still, and bent over the sleeping man on his right. What was she doing? She remained stooping for some minutes, and while she was in this attitude a new scent, unlike anything he had distinguished in the desert, became apparent; a faint, sickly, drug-like odor. Lucy rose, and stepping softly, bent over the man lying at his left hand. Again the faint, drug-like odor became apparent; again the girl seemed to be examining the sleeper closely. At length she arose, and throwing off all her caution and stealth, stepped firmly towards him, and said aloud:

"Thank God! You are saved!"

"Hush!" he whispered in alarm, "you will wake them!"

She laughed unrestrainedly, as she cut the cords that bound him.

"Before they wake, Harry, you and I will be far enough away. I have given them a sleeping draught that will keep them from interfering with us, and it rests with you whether they shall ever wake again."

Harry Broome rose, stiffly, and looked about him as a man might who is awakened from a hideous night-mare. His first impulse was to make sure of his foes, and he softly—even then doubtful of the soundness of their sleep—withdrew the pistols from their belts. Then he turned to Lucy, and gave her both his hands, silently. He could not have uttered one word of thanks or love at that moment, but his eyes were eloquent, and she accepted the unspoken offering of devotion.

Strange it was that they two should meet in the desert, and that over the bodies of his intended murderers he should renew the chain of hopes and fears and fond anticipations which had seemed, so short a time before, broken forever!

She had said the lives of the two ruffians were in his hands. He knew it as he stood and gazed upon them, lying as helpless at his feet as he had lain at theirs. There was no reason small or great why he should spare them. Their lives were forfeit to the law a hundred times. When they awoke their first movement would be to take his life, and Lucy's. His brow grew very black as he regarded them. Lucy watched and waited.

Twice he raised his pistol in his hand, and pointing it at one of the sleepers, glanced along the shining barrel. Twice his hand sank slowly by his side, and the trigger was untouched. At last he made his decision, and replaced the weapon in his belt.

"We will leave them to God!" he said. "Let us mount and ride, for I cannot trust myself to look on them again."

And they mounted and rode, taking the gamblers' horses with them. The gray, cold light of early morning was stealing out of the East, and slowly driving back the night, as they turned their horses' heads towards the western border of the desert. The alkali dust rose in clouds about them as they galloped through the dreary plain, and the desert lay before them in all its grim desolation. But not all the feverish conceptions of celestial bliss that Henry's brain had given birth to under the Shadow of Death, equalled the ecstacy of that morning ride across the repulsive alkali plains of the Forty Mile Desert.

*　　　*　　　*　　　*　　　*　　　*

The sun was high in the heavens when Mr. Cobbins awoke, feeling dizzy and queer, as though he had been drinking hard on the previous night. It took him a minute or two to collect his thoughts, and remember where he was, and what brought him there. Having succeeded in this, he sat up and looked around for the prisoner. There was no prisoner there. Mr. Cobbins sprang up and uttered a yell, which had the effect of rousing his partner, and in another minute they were both on their feet, interrogating each other as to what had happened, and cursing furiously.

After the first feeling of amazement at Broome's escape was over, and the consternation caused by the discovery that their horses had been taken, had somewhat passed off, the men began to regard each other with a rising suspicion. Was it possible thought Belto, that his partner had played him false? He, remembered now that Cobbins had prevented him from shoot. ing Harry at Lucy's house. Was there a conspiracy between him and the captive?

Could it be, thought Mr. Cobbins, that Belto had been bribed by the prisoner? Had they made an arrangement together? He recalled the affair at Kill-me-Quick, and it appeared to him now that Belto had not played with his usual skill and caution on that occasion. Was it possible that his partner had plotted to throw him off, and go in with the stranger?

The result of these cogitations was that the men regarded each other distrustfully, and that from that moment Cobbins watched Belto, and Belto kept a vigilant eye on Cobbins. But neither was inclined to force the matter to an open quarrel at that time, the instinct of self-preservation being uppermost for the moment. So they set out, grumbling and sullen, to walk back out of the desert.

The sun was very hot, the ground was very hot, the air was burning, the dust was stifling. The men were in no condition to make great exertions, for though ordinarily hardy they were both weakened by incessant dissipation, nor had they entirely recovered from the shock of the railroad accident. Towards noon they were compelled to rest, and endeavored to recruit their energies with the remainder of the whisky. As they were sitting moodily, Belto happened to look up, and behold, there were the green fields and the trees, and the rippling water of a running stream, within half a mile of them. He uttered an exclamation of surprise and pleasure, and hastily resumed his journey. Cobbins had seen the welcome objects by this time, and followed him. They walked and walked, until both were sure they must be near the edge of the desert. They examined the horizon, and there was nothing to be seen but burning sand and dazzling alkali. Then they knew that they had been deceived by the mirage, and their spirits fell.

As the day wore on a hot wind rose, and blew the sand about in clouds, at times obscuring the view so completely that they were forced to pause. In the distance they could see tall columns of sand, caught up by the whirlwind, carried spirally sixty or a hundred feet into the air, and then swept, in a gigantic waltz, across and about the desert. At times these moving pillars approached so near as to cause them serious alarm, but they escaped that danger, and struggled on their way.

Presently dark clouds began to gather over the hills in one direction. They seemed to spring into existence out of a previously cloudless sky, and to hurry up as though urged by a furious wind, or attracted by magnetic forces. Blacker and heavier they massed together over the low hills. The wind sank suddenly. The sun poured down fiercely. Then a red flash darted from the bosom of the black cloud-bank, and the thunder pealed over the desert. Great drops of rain, swept by a cold wind that came from the hills, pattered upon the parched ground; then a heavy shower, quick and short, was dashed upon the plain. Then the red lightning flashed, and the thunder rattled and crashed, and the rain fell, and the sun shone, all together. In a few minutes this strange storm was over, and the clouds vanished as quickly and as mysteriously as they had appeared.

As the partners grew more fatigued and disgusted, they naturally became more irritable and quarrelsome; and as they had exchanged very few words since the morning, their mutual suspicions had ripened while they brooded. Moreover they were hungry, and all the world knows that hungry men are angry men. Perhaps the thunderstorm had affected their nervous systems, or the sun had unduly heated their brains also. But whether from any of these causes, or all these causes combined, the partners were both rapidly approaching an aggressive condition, and it needed but a slight spark to start them into a blaze. That spark was supplied by Mr. Belto's demand for the whisky bottle, which Mr. Cobbins carried. The latter responded to the demand by remarking that he wasn't going to let Belto drink *all* the whisky. Belto retorted by the assertion that his partner was always a hog over his liquor, but that this belonged to him also, and he proposed to have his share. This was a threat, and was met by a defiance. Belto was thoroughly angry by this time, and said something about what he would do if the whisky was not forthcoming. Cobbins laughed in his face, fiercely and tauntingly. Belto felt for his pistol, and finding that it was gone, drew his knife. His partner's weapon was out on the instant.

Then they looked one another full in the eyes, and began to taunt each other with treachery. All the suspicions of the morning found vent in bitter accusations, mingled with awful threats and tremendous oaths. They were baiting one another, and working themselves up. At length Cobbins grew weary of this, and hurled an epithet at his partner which is always accepted, among such men, as an unpardonable insult. Belto rushed upon him, and the fight began.

The men were well matched, for though Belto was much the heavier, Cobbins' proficiency with the knife made up for the difference in weight. Both were desperate, both were cool, both were bent on killing. The combat was not long, however, for neither sought to escape wounds. Cobbins was the more scientific fighter, and after some cuts and thrusts had been exchanged, he threw himself apparently open for a moment. Belto seized the opportunity, sprang forward with a ferocious cry—and fell with his heart split in two by his opponent's knife, but plunging his own weapon, as he fell, with a last convulsive thrust, deep into his partner's thigh.

The party from Shoo Fly that went in pursuit of the gamblers, after Lucy's return, found Belto's body lying alone on the desert, but a bloody trail led them from the scene of the combat to where, some half a mile away, Cobbins had fainted and died the wallet grasped in his stiff hand, showing that his last act in life had been to plunder the corpse of his companion.

5

EPILOGUE.

A CHRISTMAS VISIT.

Christmas in San Francisco. The winds which make Summer sojourn in the metropolis of the Golden State almost a martyrdom, had died away. The pleasant Autumn weather, so soft, so bright, so genial, had become a memory. The rain was pouring steadily down, and everything was muddy and damp and uncomfortable. Not quite everything though. In a parlor of one of the principal hotels a young couple were seated, conversing quietly. They were evidently man and wife, and they had evidently assumed that relation toward each other very recently. The young husband was Harry Broome. The bride was Lucy Draper.

They were talking of the past.

" Did you not care for me," he said, " before that dreadful affair in the desert?"

She looked into his eyes fondly as she answered.

"Not very much, Harry, I think. It seems to me that I first realized how dear you were to me, at the moment when you rose from between those wretches, and looked at me."

" But I said nothing to you on that occasion, did I?" asked Harry, smiling.

" No, you *said* nothing. But you *looked* a great deal," rejoined Lucy.

A knock at the door, a waiter with cards—"*Mr. and Mrs. John Rutter.*"

Harry handed the cards to his wife without speaking. She glanced at the name, flushed a little, and turned, to find him regarding her with some anxiety. Placing her hand in his, she whispered softly—

" Let them come up, dear. There is no danger now."

FINIS.